A Highlander in Her Past

TRISH'S STORY

A MACKAY CLAN LEGEND
BOOK FOUR

MAEVE GREYSON

MAEVEGREYSON.COM
Magical Romance Sizing Through Time

This is a work of fiction. Names, characters, places, and incidents are either the product of the author's imagination or are used fictitiously, and any resemblance to actual persons living or dead, business establishments, events, or locales, is entirely coincidental.

A Highlander in Her Past

COPYRIGHT © 2013 by Maeve Greyson

Contact Information: maeve@maevegreyson.com

Author Maeve Greyson LLC

55 W. 14th Street

Suite 101

Helena, MT 59601

Learn more about Maeve and her books at https://maevegreyson.com/

Second Edition – July 2023

Published in the United States of America by Author Maeve Greyson LLC

CHAPTER
ONE

"Mother said—"

"I dinna care what your mother said, Keagan. I'm no' in need of a wife!" A familiar tingling tickled beneath Maxwell's scalp as he stomped deeper into the tower library. "And ye'd best leave off trying to plant your wishes into my mind. Both your parents will tell ye it canna be done." Damn the headstrong boy. Relentless as his father and wily as his mother.

Keagan perched in front of the center worktable, a polished bronze plate mounted between an upright pair of blackened iron posts balanced between his hands. The young boy pulled the mirror closer to his chest as Maxwell approached.

His ever-widening eyes sparked with determination as he let go of the mirror long enough to rub the back of one hand across the end of his nose.

"I said leave it, Keagan!" Maxwell smacked an open palm atop the worktable.

The resounding *thwack* echoed through the high-ceilinged room. The force set the flames to dancing atop the table candelabra. Keagan's nose was itching. Maxwell recognized the ominous telltale sign. The boy's magic had shifted into the hell-bent surge of a warhorse spurred toward battle.

"All ye have to do is look. What harm could befall ye just by looking?" Keagan sat a bit straighter on the stool while tapping a finger against the scrying disk. A conniving smile lit up his cherubic face as he scooted the mirror closer to Maxwell.

Maxwell closed his eyes and scrubbed the roughened knuckles of one hand across his forehead. They needed to be done with this madness and get to the stables. The last thing he needed today was Faolan's surly remarks about always having to wait whenever he sent Maxwell to fetch his son. The pulsating tingle evaporated away from the base of his skull. Good. Maybe the boy realized he was in no mood for this foolishness.

With a relieved huff, Maxwell dropped his hand to his side and opened his eyes. *God's beard.* A startling image, a moving image, stared back at him from the highly polished scrying plate.

Maxwell sagged against the table, gripping its edge. As the woman in the mirror winked, then laughed, an uneasy weight of premonition settled heavily in his gut. With his gaze locked on the scrying plate, Maxwell sank onto a nearby stool.

Pushing an opened spell book and quill aside, Keagan chuckled as he propped his ink-smudged chin atop his folded hands. "She looks to be a fine woman. Do ye not think so?"

Maxwell glared at Keagan over the top of the mirror. "What have ye done, Keagan?" The words almost stuck in his throat.

"I found ye the perfect match. What do ye think?"

What did he think? How the hell could he think when faced with a moving reflection trapped inside a damn mirror? No. Not just a moving reflection. A woman. A woman whose image set his heart to pounding and knotted his gut with anticipation. And why? It was just a woman. It wasn't as though he was a mere lad who'd never known the pleasure of a woman's softness.

Maxwell waved a hand toward the image as though trying to shoo it away. "I think ye'd best send her back to wherever ye found her and leave well enough alone. I can tell by the look of her that she's no' from this time. Nothing good can come of this. Send her away and be done with it."

A disappointed frown puckered Keagan's mouth as he shook his head. "It took me a fortnight to find her for ye. Ye need to look at her again."

Look at her again? Her vibrant image was forever burned into his mind. Maxwell stole another glance at the mirror searching for a flaw to puncture Keagan's plans. "Aye. I'll admit she's quite lovely— if ye like that sort of woman." Triumph surged through Maxwell as Keagan's shoulders slumped in disappointment. That would do it. He'd pick apart the boy's plan until the lad was convinced all this matchmaking business was more trouble than it was worth.

"What do ye mean? *That* sort of woman?"

Settling his weight more comfortably on the stool, Maxwell motioned toward the woman. "I canna tell for certain but look at her hair. Her curls are shorn close to her head." Maxwell waggled an eyebrow. "Do ye think she's been ill?" He paused, relishing the uncertainty settling in Keagan's eyes. "Or infested?" Maxwell leaned forward, a firm sense of victory tingling across his flesh. He'd have the boy convinced in no time. "And she's no' wearing any adorn-ments. Does she care so little for herself?"

"Care so little for herself?" A puzzled look darkened Keagan's face as he slid off the stool and walked to Maxwell's side. Resting his hand on Maxwell's shoulder, he pointed at the image. "Look there. She's got a gemstone hanging about her neck. She's just modest in her finery." He frowned as he leaned a bit closer, squinting as he studied the image. "And I think her hair is just pulled back like Mother does when she's not in the mood to fuss with it."

Sliding out from under Keagan's hand, Maxwell rose and headed toward the door. "No, Keagan. I think yer magic happened upon an unlikely match. Best leave it to the Fates."

Keagan stared at the mirror one last time then cut his gaze back at Maxwell. With a stiff nod and a humorless smile, he dismissed the image with a wave of his hand. "Perhaps ye are right."

Maxwell paused at the doorway, resting his hand atop the coolness of the weighty iron latch. He couldn't quite put his finger on it but something just wasn't right. Keagan hadn't put up much of an argument. Had the lad given up so easily? "So ye will leave it?"

Keagan crossed his arms over his narrow chest and bobbed his head in a curt nod.

Maxwell tried to shake off a distinct weight of foreboding as he yanked open the chamber door. "Good."

"Aye, Uncle Maxwell. I'll be leavin' it to the Fates."

Maxwell spun and studied the boy's smug look. What the hell did he mean by that?

CHAPTER

TWO

"Hello, my minions!" Trish paused, peering over the strategically stacked packages in her arms. "Where are you, my little heathens?" Trish bounced her backside against the heavy door, forcing it shut against the persistent push of the frigid Highland wind.

Balancing the boxes on one hip, she looked up the winding stone staircase to the right of the entry hall. Nothing stirred but the colorful tapestries hung along the rough gray surface of the ancient stone walls. She eased a step closer to the base of the stairs, anticipation building like a boiling teakettle about to whistle. Trish held her breath and angled an ear toward the archway. Any minute now a dozen thundering feet should echo from the upper region of the castle. She listened closer. Nothing. How odd. Especially for her favorite bunch of imps.

Sucking in enough air to force a shout into every level of the keep, Trish bellowed another enticement, "I don't hear you, my little curtain climbers. I guess I'll have to take all these gifts back to the store since there is no one here who wants them."

She slid the armload of brightly wrapped bundles onto the

marble-topped entry table, pausing once she'd relieved herself of the arm-numbing load to drum her fingers on the uppermost box. Surely the promise of gifts would get the little rascals moving.

A shrill war whoop cracked the silence, bouncing off the beams of the high ceilings, and was followed by repeated booms of multiple slamming doors. The pounding of a herd of scurrying feet became louder as they emerged from the depths of the second floor.

"Auntie Trish! Auntie Trish!" A cacophony of excited shrieks and the thud of little bodies ricocheted down from the second floor, nearly rattling the stained glass windows in their casings.

"Do you have any idea how many times I have told them *not* to run down that staircase?" Nessa heaved a tired sigh as she waddled through the stone archway.

"Oh, give me a break, Nessa. You know as well as I do that any kind of staircase holds a special kind of magic for kids." Joy filled Trish's heart to near bursting as she spotted the first curly mop of silvery blond hair bouncing around the corner. "Especially with your lively bunch." Amazement raised Trish's hand to the base of her throat. "My gosh, they've grown at least a foot since the last time I was here."

The boisterous jumble of young children spilled down the last bend of the staircase like bees swarming from the hive. The chattering group surrounded Trish with a jostling flurry of sharp little elbows and flying hands vying for her embrace.

"Whoa, minions!" Trish laughed as the crashing wave of little bodies scooted her sideways across the floor. "Hold on, you wicked little beasts. You know I've got enough hugs for all." Trish buried herself in the wiggling bunch, swallowing hard against the lump of emotions threatening to cut off her air. Damn, she had been away too long this time. They weren't babies anymore. She sucked in a deep breath, inhaling the squeaky clean scent of each and every child then closed her eyes against the sting of happy tears. She had missed this rowdy bunch.

Straightening from the stranglehold of little arms, Trish rested a hand atop the nearest tousled head. "My goodness, I have never smelled such a clean bunch. Have all of you already had your baths for the evening?"

Nessa cleared her throat and five pairs of little eyes swiveled in her direction. "Your minions will be going to bed early tonight...to *think* about the results of poor choices."

A collective groan rose from the group as they pressed closer to Trish. The boy closest to Trish's elbow looped a spindly arm tighter around her waist as he pouted a quivering lower lip toward Nessa. "But Momma, we want to stay up and visit with Auntie Trish." His wide eyes glistened with unshed tears as he snuggled his curly brown head up under Trish's arm. "And besides, it was Ramsay's fault. He tricked us. Ye know he's the troublemaker."

Trish frowned. Where *was* Ramsay? Waving a finger through the air, she pointed at the top of each little head, silently adding up the number of bodies milling around her. *Three...four...five.* Five? Trish touched the curls of each slightly damp head and called out their names. "Catriona, Beathan, Hamish, Sawny, and Gordon. Where is my sixth minion? What have you done with my Ramsay?"

Catriona and Beathan tightened their little mouths into unhappy flat lines and shuffled a few steps back. "Auntie Nessa told Cousin Ramsay not to come down from the north tower 'til he cleaned up the terrible mess."

Trish turned to the three boys still crowding her elbows. "What did your brother do this time?"

All three boys glowered dark looks at Catriona and Beathan, then turned solemn faces toward Nessa and clamped their mouths shut.

Wow. What a reaction. Trish scanned the guilt-ridden faces of all five children. Nessa's sons never clammed up when it came to sharing their latest adventures with Auntie Trish. The little mischief makers always included her in the excitement no matter how far away she might wander with her latest archeological dig. They all had her cell phone number and if they couldn't sneak a call, their text messages kept her updated on every detail. Fiona and

Brodie's twins were never far behind either when it came to keeping her entertained. The wild crop of MacKay youngsters filling this corner of the Highlands invariably had some sort of mayhem cooking and Trish loved it when they kept her abreast of the latest plot.

"What did they do this time, Nessa?" Trish didn't miss how the patches of red staining the boys' cheeks grew brighter with each passing moment. Whatever the bunch had done this time, it must've been really bad.

"Never mind." Nessa herded the children into a tighter cluster and pointed them toward the staircase. Casting a meaningful look back over her shoulder, she locked gazes with Trish. "I'll talk to you about it later."

Nessa returned her attention to the sheepish group of children milling about and directed them with a stern jerk of her chin. "As for all of you"—Nessa took another step toward the stairway and jabbed a pointing finger toward the second floor—"you've finished your hellos with Auntie Trish. Now back up those steps and into your rooms. Your punishment still stands."

A disappointed groan floated up from the youngsters as they wilted before Trish's eyes. Poor munchkins. Always into something. Surely, whatever they had done couldn't have been all that bad.

The children shuffled up the staircase, ascending the steps with about as much speed as thick molasses in the dead of winter. Hamish paused at the back of the group, his small hand white-knuckling the top of the mahogany banister. "I just want ye to know, Momma." He puffed out his chest a bit farther and sniffed in a hitching breath. "Ye don't have to worry about me listening to Ramsay no more. I'll ne'er follow his lead again."

"Anymore, Hamish. You won't listen to Ramsay *anymore*." Nessa graced her son with a loving smile as she nodded toward the second floor again. "I'm glad to hear that you're going to think for yourself from now on rather than let Ramsay talk you into foolhardy choices. Now up to your room, young man. Your father will be home in a few days and he's going to have a nice long chat with all of you about your behavior today."

Hamish's face grew even longer. "Yes, Momma." His shoulders slumped as he ducked his head and joined the rest of the group. Moving as one, the unhappy children huddled together and continued up the wide stone steps winding against the curved wall.

Trish shook her head as Nessa turned to face her. "What in the world did they do this time?" Her untouched gifts for the children caught her eye, dampening her glad-to-be-back mood. "You didn't even let them have their presents."

Nessa blew out a weary sigh as she rubbed the inside corners of her eyes. "They can have their gifts tomorrow. *After* they've had enough alone time to mull over the error of their ways."

Trish studied Nessa's drawn weary face. Nessa looked like crap. Apparently, mothering the brood of Clan MacKay was quite a strain of late. "By the way"—Trish nodded toward Nessa's rounded middle—"have you found out how many or which flavor you're going to have this time?"

"Just one, thank goodness." A glowing smile brightened Nessa's tired face. "And we're having a little girl. Catriona's very excited about increasing the ranks of the females."

"I don't blame her." Out of the corner of her eye, Trish noticed a slight movement behind the enormous tapestry covering the archway leading to the north tower. Taking care to turn so her body blocked the view of the small brown boots peeping out from under the golden fringe of the hanging, Trish unbuttoned her jacket and fanned it wide like a pair of outspread wings. "Whew! Isn't it kind of warm in here? I figured this late into December, the castle would be much cooler." There had to be a way to get Nessa out of the entry hall so Ramsay wouldn't be discovered.

Nessa swiped a few damp curls away from her forehead. "Sorry. Someone must've turned up the heat." Pulling a crumpled hankie from the side pocket of her shirt, Nessa pressed it against her throat. "I figured it was just me. The bigger I get, the more my personal thermostat gets out of whack. I bet I could heat up the entire tip of Scotland." Nessa bent sideways and motioned toward Trish's lone suitcase leaning against the curved legs of the entry table. "Are Dougal's clothes in there too? The two of you are certainly traveling light these days."

Dougal. *Ugh.* Nessa would start the visit with *that* topic. Trish shucked off her jacket and turned a bit, checking for the toes of the boots under the tapestry. Nothing appeared but the clean gray slab of stone flooring stretching beneath the arch. *Good boy. Stay out of sight until I can get rid of your mom and we can talk.* Tossing her jacket onto an ornately carved wooden bench, Trish ignored the particulars of Nessa's question. "You know me. I always travel light." Maybe if she didn't acknowledge the part about Dougal, Nessa would move on to another subject.

Nessa didn't. "Oh, Trish." Nessa threw her hands up in the air. "I thought you and Dougal were serious. I already had a spring wedding envisioned for the private garden."

Well dammit. Nessa never did know when to butt out. Trish snorted a silent laugh. That's one trait she and Nessa shared. They both enjoyed meddling in each other's business. "*Dougal* was serious. Not me. You know settling down in one spot for a cozy family life isn't my thing. There's still a lot of world I want to see."

"But the way you love kids." Nessa waved toward the staircase. "Don't you want to settle down and have a few dozen of your own?"

Trish swallowed hard against a sudden bitter lump rising in the back of her throat. She didn't have the heart to tell Nessa the cold hard facts: long ago doctors had dashed her dream of having children and refused to give her the slightest hope. Forcing a grin to her lips, Trish waved a hand toward the staircase. "Why should I go through the pain and aggravation of having my own kids when I've got the best of both worlds with yours?"

Trish backed against the forest scene tapestry covering the archway and nudged against the child-sized lump protruding from the woven reddish-brown buttocks of a slightly threadbare stag.

Damn, the boy is stubborn...and reckless. She smiled wider and nodded toward Nessa's stomach. "Besides, you look like the poster child for exhaustion. Think about it. I've got the best part of this deal. I get to play with the feisty munchkins while you have to be the mean old mom and make sure they're properly trained to charm the world."

Nessa's brows knotted over her tired eyes. "You have such a way with words. With a friend like you—"

"Now, Nessa." Trish rushed over and wrapped an arm around her friend's slumping shoulders and pulled her into a hug. "You know how much I love you. You're the sis I never had."

Nessa huffed and grudgingly returned the hug. "So, out with it. What happened between you and Dougal?"

"Nope." Trish shook her head. She wasn't about to get sucked into a relationship tell-all session until she found out what the boys had done to enact such a strict punishment. Besides, there wasn't much to tell. Dougal had been a nice enough guy but that was it. After the initial excitement of the first meet wore off, any time spent with Dougal grated on her nerves. The man had revealed himself to be an insufferable bore. If she needed a path to unbearable *yawndom,* she would bury herself in the college computer lab and code all her archeology notes for filing. *Yuck.* That thought triggered an involuntary shudder.

Trish rubbed an elbow against the tapestry at her back. *Good.* Ramsay had finally retreated. Meeting Nessa's gaze, she crossed her arms and patted a foot against the stone floor. The clicking tap of the toe of her boot echoed with a sharp report through the high-ceilinged hallway. "We're not talking about my failed relationship with Dougal until you tell me what the marauding curtain climbers of Clan MacKay did to incur your wrath."

"Magic." Nessa spat the word as though it burnt her tongue.

"Magic? Is that all?" Trish leaned against the doorframe, teetering back and forth while she peeled away the uncomfortable leather boot. She wiggled her toes and stretched out the uncomfortable seam of the tortuous sock that had embedded itself into her flesh.

Trish groaned aloud at the instant relief her poor toes transmitted to her brain. *Whew! She really needed to get rid of those heels. Comfort was so much more important than style.* Lifting her gaze from her much happier toes, she motioned toward the shattered remnants of a crystal globe encased in a well-lit curio cabinet. "Those boys have been doing magic since they were just a few weeks old. It's their heritage. You'd think you and Latharn would be used to it by now."

"Not time travel." Nessa hissed between tightly clenched teeth.

Trish straightened, hopping on the remaining high-heeled boot and stumbling toward the wooden bench fitted into a stone niche beside the doorway. "Time travel? Seriously?"

"Seriously."

"Wow." Trish kicked off the boot and pulled both feet up into her lap, relaxing yoga-style against the back of the seat. "Um. Where...or I guess the more appropriate question would be *when*?"

Nessa lowered her swollen body onto the bench beside Trish, closing her eyes as she leaned against the throw pillow threatening to squish out from behind her back. "Nowhere...or when. Luckily, Ramsay botched the spell. He claimed his cousin broke his concentration."

"I see." Trish frowned at the gently moving tapestry to her left. Hopefully, if Nessa noticed the wavering cloth, she would think it was just stirring due to heated air flowing from the free-standing heater positioned nearby.

Time travel. Ramsay had always been fascinated with the past, almost obsessed with the need to know every detail of his ancestors' lives. "Not that it matters, but which cousin did he blame? Usually, Catriona is the level-headed one of the group that catches all the heat. Was she the one who ratted them out?"

Nessa nodded without opening her eyes. "Yes. Thank goodness our little Catriona was once again the voice of reason." Flexing her spine, a pained expression darkened Nessa's face as she massaged her knuckles up and down her lower back. "Trouble is...when she forced her way into the boys' magical ring, the energy of the spell had to go somewhere and they nearly blew the roof off the northern tower."

"Is *that* what caused that gray cloud to settle across the entry bridge?" Trish massaged her thumbs into the balls of her feet. "I thought it was a little late in the season for an early evening fog."

"Yep." Nessa slid to the edge of the seat and hefted her weighty girth up from the bench with an awkward hitching launch. Pausing once she'd gained her footing, she closed her eyes and flexed her shoulders, still working her fingers up and down the base of her back. "The roof of the library tower is now hanging by a thread and half the blocks from the farthest parapet have been reduced to dust."

An involuntary shiver stole across Trish's flesh. *Holy cow.* Ramsay had outdone himself this time. Speaking a bit louder while she risked another glance at the now motionless tapestry, Trish slowly unfolded her legs. "Sounds like they definitely pushed the envelope this time." Wiggling her toes back into the persecution of her boots, Trish grimaced as she forced the tight leather heels back into place on her aching feet. "I didn't hear a second explosion so I'm assuming Latharn doesn't know that in a single afternoon, his sons destroyed a part of the castle that's survived centuries of enemy attacks and extremes of Highland weather?"

"Oh, he knows." Nessa waddled toward the wide stone archway connecting the entry hall to the larger main room making up the first floor of the keep. "According to Ramsay, his father's angry roar shook the remaining walls of the room even before the dust settled. Apparently, even though Latharn is currently meeting with historians in Ireland, he sensed the displacement of the energy blast and made certain his sons *felt* his displeasure."

"In other words"—Trish cringed as she danced her pant legs back down in place over her boots—"they're gonna get it when Daddy gets home."

"Pretty much," Nessa agreed.

CHAPTER
THREE

Trish raised the battery-operated lantern higher, increasing the diameter of the glowing blue-white circle of light pushing back the darkness. She slid her feet in slow, searching steps, brushing the soles of her boots across the cluttered, uneven flooring. She kicked aside odd-shaped chunks of debris from Ramsay's blast earlier in the day. Hopefully, for the boys' sake, Latharn would delay his return from Ireland. The man had a terrible temper when adequately provoked. He needed time to cool off before he witnessed all this damage and meted out additional punishment to his sons.

"Dammit!" Trish stumbled back and lowered the lantern, revealing the jagged-edged block of immovable stone she'd just hit with her toe and whammed into the side of her knee. Latharn would tan Ramsay's butt for wreaking so much destruction. Propping against the wall, she massaged the sting from her leg and set the lantern atop the broken masonry. The glowing orb revealed the floor of the hidden tunnel leading to the scene of the crime was cluttered with various chunks of castle debris. Trish swallowed hard against the uneasiness drying out her mouth. Maybe Ramsay needed a good spanking. It was a wonder one of the children hadn't been killed.

The faint swish of a sweeping broom echoed with a hitching rhythm somewhere deeper in the darkness. Trish cocked her head and listened closer, smiling as the muffled sound of a child's voice periodically interrupted the whooshing scrape of the broom. Nessa would tan the boy's hide if she heard Ramsay using such colorful language.

Scooping the lantern off the chunk of stone, Trish held it even with the level of her knees and concentrated on placing each foot in a safe spot among the wreckage. *Geez, what a mess.* How in the world did they expect an eight-year-old boy to clean up all this by himself? A soft popping hiss echoed through the tunnel followed by the distinct smell of sulfur.

"Ramsay! I said ye were not to use your magic." A deep voice shook through the walls of the tunnel, spilling stone dust down from the rafters.

A trembling young voice quickly squeaked out, "Sorry, Da."

Trish couldn't resist a smile. Apparently, Latharn didn't have to return from Ireland to monitor his son's progress with some sort of magical ward. Ramsay better tread lightly or Latharn would zap the boy's mischievous little butt before returning from the emerald isle.

The beam of light shining out from the lantern finally reached the end of the tunnel, revealing a black metal door barely hanging from the archway by a single bent hinge. White oxidation, as though the door had survived an extreme blast of heat, framed the edges of the thick metal slab. The gray-white scorch marks trimmed the inky black square like a border of ragged lace.

Holy crap. Trish traced a fingertip along the ancient curlicues and intertwined whorls forming the endless Celtic knot welded to the center of the door. The signet of the ancient magical seal. Blown right off its hinges. Trish shook her head. Nessa was right. They had to get Ramsay under control.

Trish inhaled a shaking breath. Ramsay was first born of Nessa and Latharn's quadruplets. Not only had he always been the most stubborn, but he was also the most gifted of the four in the ways of magic.

Trish squeezed her way around the partially opened door, holding her breath as she moved to keep from brushing against its edges. The way the thing teetered against the one remaining hinge; it could crash to the floor at any time. *Dammit, Ramsay.*

She brushed crumbs of stone dust from her hands and clothes then raised the lantern higher in the air. The rascally eldest son of the MacKay brood had always held a little tighter hold on her heart than the rest of the entertaining bunch. But this time, with all this damage, Trish doubted she'd be able to sweet talk Latharn and Nessa into an early parole for the boy. Poor Ramsay was doomed.

A blue-white glow from several strategically placed lanterns revealed the damage deeper in the room. Trish hooked the metal handle of her lantern on an iron rod extending from the first partition of the floor to ceiling bookcase creating one of the walls.

Leather-bound books and partially burned sheaves of parchment littered the stone slab flooring. Ceremonial daggers, scrying bowls, and iron candelabras peeped out from between fluttering piles of torn yellowed pages. A biting blast of frigid night air invaded the dimly lit room. Trish hugged her jacket tighter around her as she peered closer at the night sky-filled gaping hole where a solid stone wall once stood. *Yep. Ramsay outdid himself this time.*

Speaking of Ramsay—Trish scanned what part of the room she could see from the weak light shining from the scattered lanterns. Where was the boy?

"I'm over here, Auntie Trish."

"And how many times have you been told not to listen to other people's thoughts?" Trish homed in on the sullen voice coming from behind an overturned work table.

A despondent sigh echoed up from the rubble as a dust-streaked face slowly rose above the edge of a broken board. "Sorry, Auntie."

Ruffling his hands through spiked tufts of burnt orange hair, Ramsay shook off bits of plaster and stone like a dog shaking off water.

"What happened, Ramsay?" Trish stepped over the broken spokes of a shattered stool and gingerly settled down onto an enormous chunk of displaced wall protruding from the hearth. "You know you're not supposed to play with magic when your father's not here to help you."

"I was not *playing*." Clear blue eyes flashed beneath a pair of reddish-blond brows as Ramsay threw his broom to the floor. "I had everything all figured out until stupid Catriona spoiled it all."

Trish brushed bits of rubble from the spot beside her on the stone ledge. "Come. Sit down here." Trish patted the stone and urged him forward. Maybe she could talk some sense into the frustrated little rascal. She and Ramsay had always been close, sort of kindred adventuring spirits. "You do realize what you did was wrong?"

Ramsay nodded while wiping the back of his hand underneath his dripping nose. "I know that next time, I won't tell Catriona where me and the boys are gonna be doing our spells."

"Ramsay!" Trish held her breath against the urge to laugh. This was serious. She admired the boy's tenacity but he had to realize he could've killed them all. "You know good and well that's not what I meant. Now, don't you?"

"I know." Ramsay's chest deflated with a dejected sigh as he scooted up onto the stone beside her.

Trish curled her arm around the boy's shoulders and pulled him close against her side. Kissing the top of his filthy head, she rocked him back and forth like she'd done when he was just a tot. "You could've been killed, Ramsay. What would I have done without my favorite minion?" Leaning back a bit and brushing more of the grayish hunks of rock and plaster from his hair, Trish tapped once on the end of his nose. "What would I have done without another fiery redhead at the table to even out the odds against the less colorful folk?"

"Ye've cut your hair so short it doesna matter what color it is,"

Ramsay glared at her with an accusing scowl as he edged out of Trish's embrace. "And 'sides, ye'd be just fine either way 'cause ye are never here anymore."

Ahh. So that explained Ramsay's attitude toward her. Trish folded her hands in her lap and stared at the boy's bowed head. She *had* been away longer this time. The dig on the Isle of Iona had kept her away from her favorite family in the Highlands longer than she had anticipated.

"I am sorry, Ramsay." Reaching out to feather her fingers through his hair, Trish's heart lurched as the boy shied away. "Aww…come on, Ramsay. You let me hug you just a minute ago. Now you're going to pout and not even let me touch you?"

"Ye had a hold a me afore I knew what ye were doin'." Ramsay thumped his heels against the stone as he sidled an angry glance in her direction.

"I see." Trish folded her hands back into her lap. So, it was going to be like that. He was going to force her to choose sides and act like an adult. "You know I have to go away at times and tend to my digs. I can't stay here and mooch off your parents all the time. As much as I would love to dump all my responsibilities and spend every day with you, it wouldn't be fair to everyone else. I've made commitments, Ramsay. You know I always keep my word."

"Ye couldha took me with ye." Ramsay drummed his heels harder, the thunking cadence of his leather boots echoed through the chamber.

Trish slid back and drummed her own heels against the rock, matching her rhythm with Ramsay's kicking bounce. "And what would your family do without you? Your mom would be totally lost. And who would Catriona pester? The rest of the boys are afraid of her."

"Ma's fixin' to have another bairn. She wouldna even notice I was gone." Ramsay's scowl remained locked on the tips of his boots, head bent, glaring at his swinging feet as if he was waiting for them to disappear.

"You know better than that." Trish cringed at the scolding tone creeping into her voice. *Yuck.* She sounded just like Nessa. Stilling her feet, she planted both hands on either side of her thighs, leaned forward, and scanned the wreckage scattered across the floor. "Is the new baby the reason you were trying to go to the past? Are you afraid you're not going to get any attention here once your little sister is born?"

"Hell no!"

"Ramsay?"

"*You* say it. I've heard ye say worse than that many times. 'Specially when ye didna know I was around." Ramsay puffed out his narrow chest, crossing his spindly arms over the grubby front of his shirt. "And I wasna tryin' to get to the past. I was tryin' to fold time and space and make it to yer dig before ye left. I was gonna surprise ye. Catriona's a stupid nosy-butt. She peeks into Auntie Fiona's paperback books. That's where she got it in her head that I was tryin' to travel back in time." Ramsay shook his head, cutting his eyes sideways to lock an irritated glare fully on Trish's face. "I hate girls."

"Really?" Trish clamped her lips into a stern flat line. If she allowed Ramsay to witness the slightest hint of her amusement, not only would it hurt his feelings but her planned lecture would fall on deaf ears. "So, does that mean you hate me? I'm a girl."

Ramsay's smudged cheek shrugged deep into his collar as he stared down at the floor. No answer. Just the sullen thudding of two little boots banging against the stone.

"Ram. Talk to me." Trish leaned closer, nudging his little shoulder with hers. She had to get him to open up or he would never listen to reason.

"I don't hate you." Came the muffled reply as Ramsay tucked his chin deeper into his dark flannel shirt. "I just hate that Catty made me look like a dummy. I know how to work my spells. I know how to match them with the wheel." Peeping up around his collar, Ramsay's blue eyes flinched into angry slits. "If she hadna come in and ruined everything, I would've shown up by your side. I wouldha surprised ye. Now it's too late and I can't prove to nobody that I know what I'm doing."

Poor Ram. Trish knew from personal experience that nothing burned worse than knowing in your heart you were capable of doing something but no one believed it but you.

"I tell you what." Trish curtailed the urge to smooth Ramsay's wild hair back behind his ears. "Once you get this mess cleaned up and you're not in trouble anymore, you can work the spell just for me and we'll travel somewhere together. How would that be?"

"I'll be a flippin' eighty-year-old man afore I get this mess cleaned up the hard way." Ramsay whacked his heels harder against the stone perch." And Ma ain't never gonna let me outta my room."

Trish bit her tongue and held her breath. She must not laugh. "Now, Ram. You know you've been in hot water before and it didn't last that long. You've survived solitary confinement to your room before."

"I canna try the spell later. Well, at least not until a whole lot later. I hafta match the wheel."

Trish frowned, scanning the shadowed floor of the dingy room and the crooked shelves still holding what few items had survived the blast. "What wheel are you talking about? I don't see any wheel. Did it get blown away or something?"

Ramsay rolled his eyes and blew out an exaggerated sigh as though he couldn't believe Trish's naiveté. "The *seasonal* wheel, Auntie Trish. Today is Winter Solstice."

"Ahh." Trish nodded. The phases of the moon and proper timing had made a huge difference all those years ago when Latharn had saved Nessa from a black-hearted sorceress. Apparently, MacKay magic drew its potency from nature and the eternal cycle of the universe. "So, I guess your spell will only work on Winter Solstice?"

"Auntie Trish." Ramsay's voice settled into a strained placating tone. "It'll work on either of the solstices or either of the equinoxes." Dragging his sleeve under his running nose, the boy sniffed as he continued. "I'm pretty sure it'll work on the fire festival too but I'm not positive."

Trish fished a tissue out of her pocket, grabbed Ramsay by the back of the head with one hand and pinched the tissue against his nose with the other. "Blow."

Ramsay narrowed his eyes over the folds of the tissue.

"Blow, Ram. You know how much it grosses me out when you wipe your nose on your sleeve."

Ramsay trumpeted a gust of wind out his nose and grabbed the tissue to finish the job himself. "I'm not a baby. I can wipe my own nose."

"Then don't act like a baby by using your sleeve and sniffing." Trish shuddered and pulled another tissue out from the depths of her pocket. "Here. Take this one for later."

Ramsay snatched the wadded tissue out of her hand and shoved it into his sporran. Running the tip of his tongue over his lower lip, Ramsay avoided Trish's gaze and stared across the room.

Trish groaned. Not good. Whenever the boy worked the tip of his tongue across his bottom lip it meant he'd shifted into plotting mode. They'd all learned to pick up on that telltale sign before Ramsay even learned to walk. "What's buzzing around in that head of yours, Ram? You haven't even gotten out of the doghouse over this..." Trish waved a hand, encompassing the chaos of the entire room from the overturned tables and emptied shelves to the tattered plaids dangling from the walls.

"I was just thinkin'." Ramsay shrugged a dusty shoulder while starting a slow rocking motion from side to side.

Grabbing the child by the shoulders, Trish forced him to sit still. "Out with it, Ram. Whenever you stick out your tongue and start rocking, you're always up to something that you generally shouldn't do."

Ramsay widened his eyes and laid a hand to his chest, failing at a weak attempt to cover the mischief beaming from his face with a look of complete innocence. "I was just thinkin' that if ye'd let me try the spell again, I could sift ye to yer room and ye wouldna have to walk through that ole dark tunnel again."

Bullshit. Trish bit her tongue against her favorite expletive, reminding herself that Ram didn't need any additions to his already colorful vocabulary. The twinkle in his eyes was a dead giveaway that he still itched to try that spell. Forcing an appreciative expression across her face, Trish slowly rose and moved a few feet away. "So, you're trying to redeem yourself by being considerate, worried that I'll be scared in the tunnel? Is that what I'm hearing?"

Ramsay nodded while the pink tip of his tongue raced back and forth across his lower lip.

Trish's conscience kicked into gear. What would it really hurt to let him try the spell? Either it would work and they'd end up in her room or he'd fail and they'd end up staring at each other across the wreckage in the gloomy library. Trish stuffed her hands deep into the back pockets of her jeans. *Damn.* She really needed to be the adult here and tell him no. Another look at the lad's expectant face and a pang of guilt shot an arrow of sympathy straight through her heart. He already felt like she'd deserted him and stayed away too long. She knew he didn't accept her excuse of a weak signal for all those unanswered text messages when her schedule had been so overloaded.

"I'd hate for ye to have to go through that dirty ole tunnel again." Ramsay leaned forward and his eyes grew rounder. "I bet there's even spiders in there."

"Spiders, huh?" Trish bit the inside of her cheek to keep from laughing. Ramsay was pulling out all his ammunition. He knew how she hated spiders. She'd probably end up regretting this but how could she tell him no? Nessa would wring her neck if Latharn's magic alarms went off and they got caught. Shifting her stance on the dusty floor, Trish nodded once in Ramsay's direction. "I'll make you a deal."

Ramsay hopped off the stone and edged a bit closer.

Trish couldn't squelch her amusement any longer. The look of anticipation lighting up the child's face was more than she could bear. With a giggle, she reached out and ruffled his hair. "Oh, Ramsay. You're such a little con artist. What would I do without you?"

"Ye'd be a very bored old woman," Ramsay noted with a solemn nod.

With a playful cuff atop the boy's head, Trish bent closer until the tip of her nose nearly touched his. "You call me an old woman one more time and I'll leave you up here by yourself—without the aid of your spell."

Ramsay wrapped his arms around Trish's neck and snuggled his face against her cheek. "Ye know I love ye, Auntie Trish. I didna mean to call ye old."

Her heart melted. Trish scooped the boy into a tighter embrace and planted a kiss atop his head. "You may be a little rat. But you're the best rat I know. You know that?"

A muffled giggle rumbled against her neck as Ramsay nodded his head.

Might as well get it over with. Trish glanced at her watch. Surely, everyone else was asleep by now; even Latharn should be asleep over in Ireland. Ramsay could spell them down into her room and then take the tunnel back up to the tower and return to attacking his mess. "Okay, Ramsay. Here's the deal. I'll let you work your spell on the condition that once we travel back to my room, you come back up here and finish your assigned punishment."

Ramsay stepped back, flattened his little hand over his heart and stood a bit taller. "I give ye my word as a MacKay."

Holy cow. The boy sounded just like his father. Trish straightened her jacket and nodded. "Okay. Let's do this." She tapped a bright-red fingernail against the face of her watch. "You've got about forty-five minutes left in your Winter's Solstice."

"Gimme your hands." Ramsay held both grubby hands palms up,

his feet spread slightly apart beneath a dusty kilt hanging at a crooked angle about his tiny hips.

Taking a deep breath, Trish settled her fingertips into Ramsay's damp little palms and forced a solemn look on her face. "Now what?" She needed to do this right. Poor Ram's feelings had been bruised enough.

"Ye have to think about yer room." Ramsay sniffed, eyed his sleeve then sniffed again as he returned his gaze to Trish's face. "Sorry. I'll blow it later." Rubbing his cheek against his shoulder, he tightened his grip on Trish's hands. "Close yer eyes and stay focused on the inside of yer bedroom. Then all ye gotta do is follow my lead. Do what I do and maybe say what I say. I don't think ye'll need to say anything but I'm not really sure. I'll have to let ye know about that part as soon as I feel the energy. 'Kay?"

Trish closed her eyes, holding her breath against a mutinous giggle threatening to break free. "Got it."

In a high-pitched voice that still managed to ring with author-ity, Ramsay swung their clasped hands higher into the air and guided them both into a slow-moving clockwise circle. "By the power of time, by the strength of space, take us to my loved one's place."

Trish kept her eyes closed; a chill shivered across her skin as Ramsay chanted the rhyme. She cracked one eyelid open and stole a peek. Nothing. They still stood in the center of the destroyed library. Still moving in the slow circle, she fully opened her eyes. "Maybe you need to say it again. Isn't there something about doing everything in threes?"

"Auntie Trish. I was *not* finished."

"Oh. Sorry." Trish tightened her eyes shut along with her mouth. *Come on, powers. Give the kid a break. He's had a rough day.* Trish matched Ramsay's careful shuffle as they continued moving in a slow circle.

"By the power of time, by the strength of space, take us to my loved one's place." Ramsay raised his voice this time, matching his

24

steps and the swing of their hands with the cadence of the rhyme. "Dammit," he muttered under his breath.

"Ram?"

"Sorry." Ramsay heaved an irritated sigh. "It shouldha worked by now. I can't figure out what's gone wrong."

Poor little guy. Trish's heart ached. She swallowed hard and straightened her shoulders with renewed determination. Even if Ramsay's spell didn't work; he at least had to know that she believed in him. Maybe she should give the chant a go. "By the power of time, by the strength of space, take us to my loved one's place." As an afterthought, she added a few lines she'd once heard Latharn use. "For the good of all, and with harm to none, so let it be spoken, so let it be done."

"Holy crap! That's it, Auntie Trish!"

A moaning roar blasted into the room, whirling around them with a gale force wind that threw them against the farthest wall. Trish grabbed Ramsay, sheltering him against her chest as their bodies flew higher into the air. Snugging her cheek against the top of the child's head, Trish struggled to open her eyes enough to see what was happening. Brilliant flashes of blue-white light forced her to bury her face in his hair, squinting them shut against the blinding arc.

The squalling energy rose to a high-pitched scream. Trish's heart hammered into her throat. The erratic rush of blood pounding in her ears drowned out all other sound. The force of the storm tore against her body, felt as if it was about to tear her flesh from her bones. If she survived this Pandora's box, she'd paddle Ramsay's butt herself.

The sound disappeared just as quickly as it had exploded into the room. The last of the gust crashed them against the stone wall before dropping them to the floor. Trish clutched Ramsay atop her body, his limp weight resting heavily against her chest. Squeezing her hands up and down his arms, Trish forced herself not to panic. Ram was entirely too still. A warm sticky wetness trickled down the side of her face as a sharp pain burst through the base of her skull.

Air. Dammit, I need air. A stabbing burn shot through her ribcage as she gasped in a shallow breath and tried to shift to her side. Trish attempted to open her eyes. *Bad move.* She closed them quickly against a wave of nausea launching her into a black spinning void. As she whirled into the darkness, Trish made out the sound of a strong deep voice over the dull roar howling in her ears.

"God's beard, Keagan. What the hell have ye done?"

CHAPTER

FOUR

"Has she stirred yet?" Maxwell eased into the room, closing the door quietly behind him.

The woman in the chair settled her needlework in her lap and glanced toward the bed. "She moans a bit but hasn't opened her eyes. I'm afraid the wound to her head might be more severe than we first thought."

Maxwell didn't doubt Ciara's fears. He'd seen such injuries during the course of battles. The outcome wasn't usually good. He drew closer to the edge of the bed, clasping his hands behind his back. "And the boy?"

Ciara smiled and picked up the cloth, pulling the looped thread taut with the needle. "The boy is fine. He's with Keagan. Apparently, the bodies of the very young are much more resilient when traveling through time."

Maxwell stared down at the pale; motionless woman cocooned among the pillows in the overstuffed bed. So delicate—just as she had appeared in the mirror. Her translucent skin reminded him of the fresh cream shimmering in the larder pans.

He leaned forward and brushed a short ringlet of her copper-colored hair back from the bandage wrapped around her head. Such a vivid shade. The lass's hair rivaled the fiery locks of the goddess Brid herself. But so short. Had the lass been punished? Had her hair been shorn close to her head as the result of some sort of crime?

"She is quite lovely. Isn't she, Maxwell?"

Maxwell returned his hands to the tightly clasped position at the small of his back and swiveled his attention to the grinning woman sitting in the high-backed chair. *Damn, Ciara.* He recognized that tone. She was up to her usual mischief. He cleared his throat. "I hadna truly noticed. I was just wondering who had cut off all her hair."

Ciara's smile widened. "If she is from the year I think she's from, she chose to cut it that short."

Maxwell turned back to the unconscious woman. Shining red hair snipped so short ye could barely brush it? *Sheer madness.* His gaze traveled down the ivory path of her throat and came up short at the enticing bit of décolleté smattered with a dusting of pale freckles. Maxwell rubbed his thumbs across his knuckles as he pressed his fists tighter against the small of his back. *Lore, her skin looks as soft as velvet.* He'd bet his favorite dagger the woman's entire body shimmered with those tempting little marks. The gods had sprinkled her skin with their favorite spices. Maxwell smiled. He had a particular fondness for just such spice. His groin tightened as he shifted his stance.

Ciara's muffled giggle interrupted his thoughts. *Damn that woman.* Maxwell cleared his throat. "What year do ye think she is from? Or did the boy finally open up to Keagan?"

Ciara set her sewing into the seat of the chair as she moved to wring out a rag in the bowl of steaming water on the table beside the bed. "All we've been able to get from the boy is his name." Her voice softened as she gently pressed the damp folded cloth against the silent woman's cheeks and smoothed it across her shoulders. "He refuses to answer any other questions until he's talked with her."

"Aye." Maxwell nodded toward the bed, wrinkling his nose

against the scent of lavender rising from the heated rag Ciara pressed against the woman's temple. He hated lavender; it brought to mind too many memories of ailing and loss. "He's a good lad. His mother probably instructed him to be careful."

The door burst open and Ramsay exploded into their presence. "What are ye doing?" He ran across the room and clambered over the end of the bed, dodging Ciara and Maxwell until he sat wedged between Trish and the wall. "Is she awake yet? Can ye tell if she is all right?"

"Be still, boy!" Maxwell leaned across the bed, grabbed Ramsay by the shoulders, and lifted him to the floor. "Your mother is ill and doesna need the likes of ye bouncing her all over her sickbed."

"She is NOT my mother." Ramsay squirmed free of Maxwell's grasp and backed against the side of the bed. With a sullen scowl, he folded his scrawny arms across his chest with an irritated yank. "And I would never hurt Auntie Trish. I know she wants me here."

Maxwell admired the boy's fighting spirit. And damn if the lad didn't look familiar, especially around his eyes. "What's your name, boy?"

Ramsay jerked his chin toward Ciara. "I told Keagan already and I know he's told *her*. It's Ramsay."

"*Her* name," Maxwell corrected in a warning tone, "is Lady Ciara. Ye will address her with respect. She is the lady of Clan MacKay."

Ramsay's arms unfolded and slid to his sides as his scowl shifted to a look of confusion. "My momma is the lady of Clan MacKay."

Uneasiness sent a warning tingle across Maxwell's flesh as he peered closer into Ramsay's face. "Name your parents, boy."

Ramsay stood a bit taller, stuck out his chest, and proudly lifted his chin. "My momma is Nessa and my da is Latharn MacKay, honored chieftain of Clan MacKay."

"Latharn?" Maxwell took a step back. *That's* why the boy looked so familiar. Twisting the wiry curls of his beard through his fingertips, Maxwell cocked his head to one side as laughter rumbled through his chest. So Latharn had survived Deardha's curse and gone on to sire this fine strapping lad. *God's beard.* Wait 'til Faolan heard the news.

Returning his gaze to the pale woman in the bed, Maxwell hooked his thumbs into the wide leather belt cinched about his waist. "And this is your mother's sister? Yer Auntie Trish?"

Ramsay turned and rested his little hand against Trish's cheek. His voice hitched a bit as though he struggled with barely controlled emotions. "She's not really momma's sister but we call her Auntie Trish 'cause she loves all of us like we belong to her." Ramsay swallowed hard and his voice fell to barely above a whisper. "And we love her too."

"You *all* call her Auntie Trish." Maxwell examined the boy with interest. Apparently, Latharn had not only survived the witch's curse, but he'd also thrived in whatever century he'd landed.

"Aye." Ramsay nodded. "Me and Hamish, Sawny and Gordon." He sniffed, started to wipe his nose on his sleeve then stopped and pulled a wadded bit of thin white cloth from the tiny fur pouch hanging from his waist. A trembling smile flickered across his mouth as he glanced at Trish and blew his nose. After wiping his nose, he shoved the crumpled rag back into his sporran. With a final sniff, he reached out and gently laid his hand on the pillow beside Trish's head. "Catty and Beathan call her Auntie Trish too. But they're my cousins, not my brother and sister."

Ciara rested her hand atop Maxwell's shoulder. "I knew Latharn had done well. Faolan will be so pleased to hear this news."

Maxwell snorted. "Aye. Latharn's done better than well. And Faolan will be more than pleased. He'll be relieved."

At that moment, Trish stirred beneath the covers, shifting her head from side to side. With a weak moan, she dragged a hand over her eyes, her pale fingers trembling. "Ramsay. Would you please turn the TV down and shut off a few of these lights? Auntie Trish's head is about to split wide open. This migraine appears to be a doozie."

Joy radiated from Ramsay's face. His mouth stretched into a wide, toothy grin. "It's not the TV, Auntie Trish. And the only kind of lights we've got in this room are bunches of candles. Ye want me to blow a few of them out?"

Trish's squinting blue eyes appeared between her spread fingers as she slowly shifted to her side. "Son of a—"

"Auntie Trish!"

Maxwell bit back the laughter threatening to spill and grabbed Ramsay by the shoulders, gently moving him to the side. "Ye would fare better if ye kept still, lass. Ye've got quite a gash across the back of your head and a fearsome bruise forming over the ribs on your right side."

Trish flinched as her hand slid away from sheltering her eyes. Lifting the blankets, she tucked her chin and peered beneath covers. "Uhm. I appear to be naked."

"Don't worry, Trish," Ciara interjected. "I'm the one who undressed you once Maxwell brought you to the bed."

Pulling the blankets higher about her neck, Trish squinted up into their faces. Her voice trembled as she mumbled, *"Thanks."* She flinched as she gently pressed her fingertips against the edges of the cloth bandage wrapped around her head. "What exactly happened?" Reaching out, she grabbed a hold of Ramsay's sleeve and pulled him over beside her. "Where are we, Ram?"

"Ye are at MacKay keep." As Trish flinched, Maxwell lowered his voice. "Ye are safe, lass. Nothing will hurt ye here."

Trish snaked an arm around Ramsay's chest and hugged him closer still. Choking out a husky whisper filled with uneasiness, Trish closed her eyes as she spoke. "I thought you said we would end up in my room?"

Ramsay looked at her with an apologetic shrug as he pointed at the highly polished stonework patterned into dark curlicues around an extremely unique hearth. "We are in your room. Kinda."

"Kinda, my—" Trish stopped, her cheeks reddening as she struggled to continue. "You better be glad it pains me to move or I would have your butt, Ramsay Alexander MacKay." Trish hissed out a pain-filled groan as she fell back against the piles of pillows.

Maxwell couldn't resist a chuckle. Lore, the woman's tongue matched the fire of her hair even when she lay weak as a kitten. "What year are ye from, boy?" Perhaps if he gave Trish a bit of time to regain her strength, she would talk more with them later.

Ramsay clamped his mouth shut and returned his arms to their stubborn position of folded over his chest.

Trish cracked open an eyelid and poked Ramsay's shoulder. "Answer him, Ramsay. You are not going to be able to single-handedly bail us out of this one. We're going to need their help."

"But I've heard of him, Auntie Trish." Ramsay turned with his hands up against his mouth as though he could hide his words. "Da told me about a man named Maxwell that was Uncle Faolan's best friend."

"And what exactly did your da say?" Maxwell hooked his thumbs back into his belt, struggling to keep from grinning. He had a pretty good idea of the words Latharn would've used to describe him. Maxwell and Latharn had never seen eye to eye because Faolan had always been closer to Maxwell than he'd been to either of his brothers. Maxwell and the eldest son of clan MacKay were best friends. Maxwell and the other MacKay siblings were not.

Ramsay remained silent.

Trish covered her eyes with her hands and deflated with a sigh. "Say it, Ramsay. I'm sure it was something brilliant."

Ramsay took a deep breath, straightened his shoulders and met Maxwell's gaze. "He said ye were a pompous arse hole that thought entirely too much of yourself."

Trish groaned and held her head as Maxwell and Ciara both snorted with laughter.

"Did he now?" Maxwell chuckled and nudged Ciara with his elbow. "Well, perhaps ye'll find I'm not nearly as big of an arse as your father described." Shoulders still shaking with silent laughter, Maxwell motioned the boy away from the bed. Poor Trish looked as if she was about to retch and every time the lad jarred the bed frame, her skin paled to another shade of sickly yellow. Maxwell bent and leveled his gaze even with the boy's. "Now, tell me. What year have ye traveled from?"

After a quick glance at Trish's pale face, Ramsay tucked his chin and mumbled a barely audible 2020.

"2020?" Maxwell repeated. *God's teeth.* A wave of uneasiness shuddered across his body. The woman and the boy had traveled back across the web of time nearly six hundred years.

"What year is this?" Trish croaked with one arm still thrown across her eyes.

"In but a few days, 'twill be the year 1425." Maxwell cleared his throat as he smoothed the sides of his unruly moustache. "Today's date is the tenth of December in the year 1424." Maxwell blew out a groaning sigh as he shook his head. "Winter Solstice."

"Can't be," Ramsay countered. "Winter Solstice is December twenty-first."

"Not in the year 1424, Ramsay," Trish rasped in a weakened voice from the bed.

Ramsay's blue eyes widened, glistening with unshed tears as he dove back toward the head of the bed. "I am so sorry, Auntie Trish. I dunno what could've happened."

Trish reached out and covered Ramsay's hand with her own. The lines deepened around her mouth but she remained silent, her other arm still draped across her eyes.

The poor woman. Maxwell edged a bit closer to the bed. His heart clenched as he caught the glimmer of a single tear as it escaped from beneath her arm and rolled down the side of her face. She had to know she was safe here until...Maxwell stole a glance at Ciara's worried face. Well. Until whenever. She and the boy would be safe until they chose to leave. "Ye have m'word that ye'll be protected here. Ye have nothing to fear. Neither you or the boy."

"Your word?" Ramsay turned from Trish and faced Maxwell with his eyes narrowed and an irritated frown pulling down the corners of his mouth. "Yer no' the laird here. What good is *your* word?"

"Ramsay!" Trish clutched the blankets against her throat, her face whitened with pain as she forced her body over to her side. "You will not be rude, young man. We are in a big enough mess without adding insults to the lot." Flinching as she pushed herself higher up in the bed, Trish swallowed hard and sucked in several deep breaths before she spoke again. "Thank you, Maxwell and Ciara, for everything. We'll need your protection until we can figure out a way to get back before we muck up anything in this century."

A strange feeling fluttered in the center of Maxwell's chest, shook his heart into skipping a beat, and made him swallow hard against a sudden lump swelling in his throat. Was it Trish's helpless situation that shook him to his core or the fact that she didn't collapse into an inconsolable bundle of weeping hysteria like most women in her situation would have done?

Maxwell didn't miss how she kept a protective arm curled around Ramsay even when it must surely pain her to do so. Trish had spirit; a delightful stubbornness shone from her soul. And damn those eyes beneath that ragged bandage, blue as sapphires but sparking with three times the fire. As he exhaled a tentative breath, Maxwell's gaze faltered a bit lower, mesmerized by the twin mounds of her ample breasts peeking over the edge of the covers. And the freckles. *Damn the woman and those teasing freckles.* Maxwell worked his tongue against the roof of his mouth. Where the hell had all his spittle gone? His mouth tasted as dry as the dust flooring the paddock. With a cough, Maxwell forced his attention back up to her pain-filled gaze. "Rest, Mistress Trish...er...Mistress?" Maxwell caught himself about to stammer. What the hell was wrong with him? "Or would ye prefer to be called by the name of your clan?"

Trish brought her knees up to her chest, tenting the blankets all about her. Massaging her temples underneath the bandage, she closed her eyes as she spoke. "Sullivan is my last name. But everyone here can call me Trish."

"Sullivan?" Maxwell's heart fell and he took a step back. Was he standing here lusting after his own great great granddaughter? *God's beard!* The very thought of it turned his stomach.

Trish barely nodded. Grabbing her head between both hands, Trish furrowed her brow against the jarring movement as she gasped. "Yes. Sullivan. Why?"

"Because Maxwell heads the Sullivans, a sept of Clan MacKay and he's wondering if the two of you share a bloodline." Ciara hid an evil grin from Trish behind the extra blanket she shook out across the bed.

Ye are a conniving, wicked woman, Maxwell mouthed to Ciara with the slightest tilt of his head.

Ciara's smile widened.

Trish gingerly slid back down into the depths of the bed without opening her eyes. "We might be related but it would be in name only." Plucking the covers up under her chin, she hissed out a pained sigh. "I was adopted. According to everything I can find I'm really a mutt from Czechoslovakia."

The tension left Maxwell's shoulders. He didn't have a clue where or what Czechoslovakia was but he knew none of his bloodline had been to a place so named. He tugged at the throw spread across Trish's legs, smoothing out the wrinkles across her body. "Rest, Trish. 'Tis the only thing that will truly heal ye." After a moment's hesitation, he barely traced a finger across the pale skin of the back of her hand. Pure velvet. Just like it looked.

The deep pained lines around Trish's mouth gradually faded as the rise and fall of her chest settled into the rhythm of shallow, easy breathing.

Ciara scooped up Ramsey's hand and looped her arm through Maxwell's elbow. With a smile and a nod at Trish's now-peaceful face, Ciara turned the males toward the door. "Come. She sleeps. Let the herbs do their work." Pressing a sharp elbow into Maxwell's ribs, she smiled up into his face. "It's good to know you two don't share a bloodline."

"Meaning?" Maxwell growled under his breath, struggling to keep his voice low.

"Meaning"—Ciara nudged Maxwell in the ribs again—"that perhaps the Fates sent Trish to you for a reason."

"What reason?" Ramsay piped up as they all squeezed through the door.

"Never mind," Maxwell answered. "Go find your cousin, Keagan."

CHAPTER
FIVE

"Ye do realize she's plotting and ye are doomed to the utter certainty of matchmaking hell?" Faolan shoved an overflowing tankard of ale between Maxwell's fisted hands.

Curling his fingers around the cool damp metal, Maxwell stared down at the scowl looking back up at him from the amber depths of the mug.

"Do ye think..." Maxwell paused, raised the tankard to his mouth, and sucked in a deep fortifying swallow. Lowering the mug, he returned his attention to the surface of the swirling brew. "Do ye think she might ha' sent for her?" Surely, Ciara hadn't dabbled with his fate. She couldn't just yank a woman from another fold of time just to see Maxwell tethered to a wife. Could she?

Faolan shrugged, his warrior's braid sliding back and forth across the top of his shoulder as he slowly shook his head. "My wife is a verra determined woman, Maxwell. Ye know that as well as I. How many times has she told ye that ye needed a wife over the course of just the past few months?"

"Too damn many to count." Maxwell drained the contents of the cup in one desperate gulp. Nearly every time he turned around, Ciara never failed to mention how much happier Maxwell would be if he married. He had survived this long without a wife. Maxwell slid the damp metal tankard back and forth along the well rubbed top of the wooden table, his gaze following the shapeless patterns formed by the trails of condensation. He didn't need a wife...or a family. Such things only led to unnecessary complications—complications he'd do just as well without.

Faolan propped his chin in one hand and drummed his fingertips atop the table with the other. "At least she brought ye a pretty one."

"She didn't bring *me* anything." Maxwell thunked his tankard onto the table as he rose from the bench.

Stalking across the room to the blazing hearth, Maxwell glared down into the glowing coals radiating beneath the flaming logs. Shimmering reds and oranges quivered and danced; heat waves undulated from their core. Vibrant colors. Mesmerizing and bright... like the shine of Trish's coppery hair when she stirred beneath the light of the candles.

"Dammit, Faolan!" Maxwell whirled from the hypnotic blaze, putting his back to the fire. "I dinna have need of a wife."

"Auntie Trish doesna want a husband either. 'Specially not one like you." Ramsay stomped into the hall; his little hands fisted against the sides of his kilt. The boy's lower lip barely quivered, matching the telltale tremble of his voice." She got here by accident 'cause I screwed up a spell. But Keagan's gonna help me find the way back so the doctors there can help Auntie Trish and make sure she gets better."

"Calm down, boy." Faolan rose from the bench, leaning forward with both hands atop the table. "And did your father never teach ye 'tis rude to listen in on other's conversations?"

Maxwell raised a hand, frowning at Faolan as he moved to Ramsay's side. "Let the boy alone, Faolan. He's just defending his aunt." He gave Ramsay's shoulder a reassuring squeeze. "A fine quality, boy. Always protect your women."

"Ramsay."

Maxwell turned and faced the archway leading to the stairs. Something was wrong. He sensed a darkness in Ciara's tone. Brow furrowed; Ciara stood twisting a towel between her hands.

Stepping out of the shadow of the stone arch, Ciara's knuckles whitened as she tightened her hold on the towel. "Ramsay. Ian has saddled the horses so the two of you can take them out for a bit of exercise. Dress warm. I've put some of Keagan's winter woolens on the peg in the bathing room. You can change your clothes there."

"Sweet!" Ramsay bolted from the room, his excited war whoops echoing to the rafters.

Maxwell waited until Ramsay's joyous cries faded to uncomfortable silence. Turning back to Ciara, he braced himself. He didn't know what news she was about to share but from the shadow of worry darkening her face, it couldn't be good.

"If we don't find a way to heal Trish"—Ciara paused, bowed her head, and drew in a slow deep breath. Lifting her chin, she swallowed hard and barely shook her head—"Ramsay will not have anyone to protect."

A sick feeling turned to lead in the pit of Maxwell's stomach. He knew Trish's color hadn't been good for the past few days but he'd hoped against all that he knew about battle wounds that his instincts were wrong this time. For once in his long, adventurous life, he hated being right. "Is there nothing we can do to save the lass? The boy will be devastated if she dies."

Ciara glanced at Faolan, then turned a thoughtful gaze to Maxwell. "Keagan has a theory."

"God's teeth, here it comes," Faolan mumbled, raking both hands through his hair.

Ciara pursed her lips and turned her back to Faolan but not before fixing him with an irritated look. "Keagan feels the reason Trish has done so poorly is because her natural magic is latent and the strength of her soul remains anchored in her original strand of time rather than staying with her physical presence in this reality. He thinks her spirit has been stretched too thin..." Ciara's voice trailed off, leaving them all to draw their own conclusions as to what would happen if Trish's spirit snapped.

"Latent magic? A soul's anchor?" Maxwell frowned and moved closer to the hearth. Ciara's disheartening announcement lent a chill to the room. "What the hell do ye mean by latent magic?"

"Are ye sure, Ciara?" Faolan asked. "This is a cruel joke if ye've chosen to stage Trish's impending death just to lure Maxwell to the altar."

"I will deal with you later for such an accusation, husband." Ciara's tone took on a dangerous pitch as she scowled at Faolan. Turning back to Maxwell, her face softened as she took a deep breath. "Those who fully embrace their mystical heritage survive time travel much better than those who do not." Ciara paused, shook out the twisted cloth in her hands, and folded it neatly into a small square. "Look how well young Ramsay did. The boy was up and around within minutes."

Suspicion tingled across the back of Maxwell's neck. Although it might be cruel, Faolan made a valid point. When Ciara made up her mind about something, she'd do *anything* to see it done. Maxwell pursed his lips and stroked his mustache as he searched her face for the truth. *Dammit.* The woman knew how to mask her emotions. God help Faolan with his wife. Maxwell nodded as he continued stroking his beard. Perhaps 'twould be safest for now to play along. How else could he gather information? "Aye. Ramsay was alert and running around with Keagan before Trish ever came to. What's yer point, Ciara?"

Ciara hugged the folded cloth to her chest and meandered slowly across the room. "Keagan feels if we can meld Trish's latent magic and her soul to another strong soul already anchored in this time, her natural powers will come to the surface and her strength will return. Her spirit needs a comforting refuge in this time."

Faolan snorted, then turned the sound into a hacking cough when Ciara shot him a warning glare.

"Ye know I have no magic, Ciara. How could my spirit be a

comforting refuge?" Maxwell backed against the stones of the hearth and crossed his arms like a shield over his chest.

"You do have a bit of magic, Maxwell, and a heart big enough to shelter another." Ciara took a step closer, wringing the cloth between her hands as she walked across the room. "Do you not recall blocking my magic when I tried to pull the wool of suggestion across your mind?"

"'Twas a reflex, woman!" Maxwell waved a hand in Faolan's direction. "Your husband nettled me with that infernal nonsense the entire time we were young lads. I finally learned to close my mind to any magical suggestion because I grew tired of stepping off cliffs and plunging me arse into the deepest parts of an icy loch."

Faolan shook with a low rumbling chuckle. "It did take him quite a while to learn to block the magic. I doused him at least every other day."

Ciara rolled her eyes and turned her back to her husband, facing Maxwell instead. "But the point is you did learn how to block the energy. You have *some* mystical powers, Maxwell. Most people do. They just don't know how to tap into it."

Maxwell scrubbed both hands over his face. So this was her plan. She knew if Trish's life was on the line, he'd have no choice but to do whatever she said. Honor demanded it. Damn, the stubborn woman and her conniving ways. How the hell did Faolan survive her? Blowing out a defeated breath, Maxwell dropped his hands to his sides. "What do ye propose we do? What does Keagan suggest?"

"Nothing as unpleasant as jumping into an icy loch," Ciara assured with a smile. "My talented son said all we must do is a simple intertwining of your souls."

"An intertwining of souls," Maxwell repeated. "May the goddess Brid protect us all," he added under his breath.

CHAPTER
SIX

Searing pain stabbed through her right side every time she sucked in a breath. Shallow breathing eased the misery until her lungs ached for more air. Trish steeled herself against the imminent pain. *Crap...this is gonna hurt.* She inhaled deeper, flinching at the now familiar agony of jagged bone tearing into tender flesh. Rolling her head to one side on the sweat-drenched pillow, Trish continued breathing in short erratic puffs. *Dammit.* Who the hell set off that jackhammer ratcheting inside her skull? The dull pound pulsed in sync with every beat of her heart. The nauseating ache drummed from the base of her neck all the way up the back of her skull and burned into the back of her eye sockets. Hot tears squeezed out from under her closed eyelids. *Son of a bitch!* Even tears hurt.

The high-pitched squeak of a door's hinges filtered through her misery. Trish eased her head to the right, struggling to pull one swollen eyelid open just a slit. "Who is it?" The words stuck in her parched throat. She croaked them free, pushed them past her cracked lips then immediately wished she hadn't. A fresh wave of pain exploded through her skull and vibrated down her spine.

"Don't talk, Auntie Trish." Ramsay's face swam into view. The weight of his tiny hand patted with a reassuring touch against her bare shoulder. "Just close yer eyes and listen. I know it hurts ye whenever ye talk or move."

What a good boy. Trish relaxed her eye closed and straightened her head back into the damp dent on the pillow. She must be getting worse. She couldn't imagine fully opening both eyes much less sitting up in the bed. Poor Ram. Before she died, she had to find a way to convince the little fellow that he mustn't blame himself. Everything happened for a reason. Apparently, this was just the way she was meant to go.

A large calloused hand scooped under her palm and gently lifted it off the pillowed mattress. Warmth. The hand supporting hers radiated a comforting warmth into her freezing hand. A second hand folded over the top, rubbing a work-roughened thumb across the ridges of her aching knuckles. Trish squeezed the hand. Whoever it was, their heat felt good, seemed to lessen the pain in her bones.

"Auntie Trish." Ramsey's voice floated through the haze of pain ravaging through her head. Trish struggled to hear it better. Ramsay's voice could be her anchor. For his sake, she had to hold on. She concentrated on the hand holding hers, mustering up enough strength to clench the calloused fingers with a trembling squeeze.

"She heard ye, lad. She just squeezed my hand."

A deeper voice? Trish's mind hitched trying to register on the soothing baritone rolling its "r's" in her ear. It wasn't Latharn. She knew his voice. Who was in the room with Ramsay?

"Auntie Trish. Keagan and I are going to join our powers and make ye feel better. Ye dinna have to do a thing but lay verra still and relax. Keagan says 'tis the only way for ye to get to feelin' better. But we gotta have yer full permission or the magic won't work."

Trish eased in another painful breath, mulling over Ramsay's words as they faded in and out of the painful fog clouding her mind. Magic. Spell. Feel better. Sounded like a definite *hell yeah* to her. Trish swallowed against the dryness scratching her throat, wincing as a sharp jolt of fresh agony sliced through her chest. If the spell didn't work, she would die. Either way, this endless torment would finally be over.

"Auntie Trish." Ramsay's voice grew louder, closer to her ear. "If ye agree to the magic with all yer heart, squeeze Maxwell's hand."

Maxwell? Confusion muddied the fog wrapped around her consciousness. Who the hell was Maxwell? A choking pressure inflamed her lungs. She needed more air. Drawing in a shaking breath, Trish focused what little strength she had into her right hand. *Lordy, the tiniest movement took so much effort.* She concentrated on the calloused hand cradling hers and squeezed.

"She agrees."

Was that Maxwell? Trish felt her body grow lighter; the pain surged with an unbearably strong stab then ebbed to a less searing throb, undulating like a cruel tormenting wave.

Light. Soothing light flooded into her mind, a golden stream of shimmering yellows and blazing oranges flowed through her, chasing away every last remnant of pain. Trish sucked in a deeper breath. Finally. A decent breath of air. She almost laughed aloud. A lungful of oxygen never felt so good. Directly in front of her, suspended against a backdrop of stars, a flowing cloud of iridescent particles swirled into the glowing shape of a smiling, bearded man. *Damn.* Had she finally died and was being greeted by a hairy angel?

Trish patted her body; her hands passed through her chest and stirred the shimmering air behind her. *Holy crap!* She must be dead. She peered closer at the man up ahead. Why did he seem so familiar?

The man's smile widened as he held out his hand. His translucent palm glowed with a blinding orb of blue-white light as though fired by a mysterious arc welder.

Trish drew closer. She'd never seen an angel before and this one seemed so...welcoming. As she floated across the starlit void, the vision of the man sharpened, focused clearer into view. Trish stopped. Since when did an angel wear a kilt...and sport a full reddish-brown beard?

The angel smiled and beckoned her forward while still holding out his hand.

He did seem nice enough. Trish floated forward a bit farther then stopped again. She couldn't leave until she had some sort of promise that someone would reassure Ramsay. "I can't go with you until I know Ramsay is okay. I don't want him to blame himself."

The man nodded agreement with a single dip of his chin, then extended his glowing hand again.

Wow. Who would've thought dying could be so painless? Trish floated forward another few feet, the closer she drew to the welcoming man; the more pleasurable the pulsating warmth felt coursing through her veins. She relaxed, took in a deep breath, and smiled back at him. He did have the nicest eyes. They crinkled at the corners whenever he smiled as though he were about to laugh aloud. And he seemed so friendly, making her feel as though she'd known him since the beginning of time.

He took a step forward, met her halfway, then bent and scooped up her hand. As Trish wrapped her fingers around his glowing palm, her vision exploded into a cloud of blinding white sparks, electrifying heat surged through her, then everything faded to black.

SEVEN

The faintest tickle teased across the end of one nostril. Trish wiggled her nose, rubbed it against the back of her hand, then buried her face into the furry warmth cradled against her head. *Pain-free warmth.* Trish dozed back into oblivion. Another tickle assaulted the end of her nose, threatening to trigger a sneeze.

Batting away the persistent offender, Trish stretched, inhaled a deep lung-expanding breath and burrowed deeper beneath the covers. She laced her fingers into the tight nest of curly hair springing against her face. *Hair?*

Trish opened her eyes to a mountainous mound of chest coated with a lush carpeting of reddish-brown hair. She sprang backward toward the far side of the bed, digging and kicking at the covers. "Who the hell are you and what the hell are you doing in my bed?"

The man didn't bother opening his eyes, just rolled toward Trish and beckoned with an extended arm. In a drowsy voice, mumbled against the pillows, he motioned toward his chest. "Ye know me, lass. Now quit yer fussin' and come over here. 'Tis wicked cold in this room and I'd planned on sleeping a bit longer."

Trish settled her back against the bone-chilling cold of the stone

46

wall, planted her feet dead center of the furry expanse of chest and shoved.

As his naked body slid over the edge of the bed, Maxwell's eyes popped open. He hit the floor with a heavy thud followed by several muttered words that Trish was fairly certain were Gaelic profanity. Rising above the side of the oversized mattress, Maxwell's sleepy expression changed to one of irritated confusion. "Dammit, Trish! Why the hell did ye do that?"

"You know my name?" Trish scooted as far back against the wall as she could manage, yanking all the covers of the bed up around her naked body and wadding them under her chin. How did he know her name? *Holy crap.* She was naked. He was naked. They'd been in bed together. *Dammit.* When had she gotten that drunk, and what the devil had she done? "Who the hell *are* you?"

Maxwell rose higher above the edge of the bed, scrubbing the heel of one hand against his eye while propping his head with the other. "I am Maxwell. Ye would think ye'd remember the name of the man who called ye away from death's door."

"Called me away?" Trish stared at the hairy, green-eyed man propped on the side of her bed. A nagging sense of having forgotten something very important gnawed at the back of her mind. He did seem a little familiar. But that still didn't explain who he was or why they were both naked in the same bed.

"Aye." Maxwell nodded, then stretched with another jaw-cracking yawn. Scrubbing his fingers through the mat of curly hair on his chest, he nodded toward the hearth. "The coals are low and the room is cold. Now, can I get back in the bed?"

"Are you crazy?" Trish stretched and grabbed an iron candle-holder off the shelf above the bed. "I may be small but don't make the mistake of thinking that I'm helpless." Waving the weighty weapon toward a plaid tossed across a chair beside the hearth, Trish pulled the covers closer about her chin. "There's a wrap. You can cover up with that while you explain who you are."

"God's beard," Maxwell grumbled as he pushed himself up from the floor. "'Tis a sorry day when a man saves a woman's life just to get ousted from a warm bed and sent to sit by a dying fire."

Wow. Trish arched her brows and bit her tongue against the desire to emit a low admiring whistle. He must not be *that* cold. She didn't attempt to look away as Maxwell paraded across the floor. Trish had to admit the man looked damn sexy...coated with a heavy dusting of reddish-brown hair or not. Leaning to the side to improve the angle, Trish followed him with her gaze. She'd always been attracted to the burly type. They cuddled better after a good romp in the sheets.

As Maxwell bent to retrieve the plaid, he grinned over one shoulder and winked. "I'm verra glad ye seem to be enjoying the view."

Trish shook herself and snapped her sagging lower jaw shut. She hadn't meant to stare *or* get lost in a fantasy trip. Brandishing the candlestick higher in the air, she motioned toward the chair. "Never you mind about what I'm enjoying. How 'bout you just sit over there and start explaining."

Maxwell's deep-green eyes sparkled with mischief as he raised his arms over his head and stretched long and slow.

Trish squirmed in the bed as she caught him watching her. She didn't know why he complained the room was cold. It felt pretty damn warm to her.

Maxwell peeped around a bulging bicep and flexed layers of hardened muscles in the reddish glow of the hearth before wrapping the plaid about his waist. With one hand and the ease that Trish would pick up a pencil, he hefted a log the size of Trish into the dying coals.

Trish didn't miss how the muscles of his back rippled as he stirred the fire. *Dammit.* How could she not remember playing in the sheets with *that?* Running her tongue across her lips, Trish frowned as she tasted chapped and broken skin. She raised her fingertips to her mouth, patting gently against the tender broken flesh stretched across her lips. "What is wrong with me?"

Maxwell crossed his legs at the ankles, folding his hands across his stomach as he leaned back in the chair. "Nothing now. But 'twas little more than a few hours ago that ye were about to meet your maker."

Trish pinched the bridge of her nose, rubbing the inside corners of her eyes. Nothing Maxwell said made sense. Bits and pieces of strange thoughts filtered through her mind. Were they memories or just bad dreams? "For my sake, could you please just start at the beginning and give me a quick rundown?"

Maxwell settled his head against the high back of the wooden slatted chair and stared unblinking at the ceiling. "The beginning. Well let's see. I suppose the beginning would be the part where ye suddenly appeared above the tables in the library of magics, in the midst of a howling wind with a young boy clenched in your arms. Ramsay survived the trip through time quite well but you were near fatally injured. Young Keagan figured out that only those who are fully blessed and active in their magic are able to survive navigating the web of time and bring their souls along with them. Ye see, young Ramsay's a magical MacKay but you, my dear, are not." Maxwell paused, inhaled a deep breath, and then continued, "So, the only way to save yer life was to intertwine yer soul and meld your latent magic to another soul's dormant gifts. Keagan said we must anchor ye to a soul in this time." Maxwell thumped his hand to the center of his chest. "That would be me."

Trish stared at the grinning man, her head pounding with the information he'd just spewed in a single breath. "You have got to be kidding."

"If ye think I'd go to the trouble of weaving a fantastical tale such as that just to get in a woman's bed"—Maxwell paused, then his eyes narrowed—"then ye'd best think again because Maxwell Sullivan has ne'er been that desperate for a woman to warm his sheets."

Trish closed her eyes, massaging her temples as she sorted through everything the man had just said. She remembered now.

Burying her face in her hands, she groaned out loud. "I can't believe I'm sitting here naked in the year 1424."

"Aye. Well." Maxwell chuckled a warm deep laugh. "Ye are doing it quite well."

Great. Just what she needed right now. A freakin' comedian. Trish raised her head, propped her elbows on her knees, and rested her chin in her hands. "You still didn't explain why the two of us woke up this morning. Together. Naked."

Maxwell scratched his chin and grinned down at his feet. "First of all, it willna be morning for quite some time. Secondly, when two souls are joined, the bodies are..." His words trailed off into suggestive oblivion.

Trish sat bolt upright. "Are you telling me we *did* it?" *Holy crap!* She hadn't forgotten the details of a sexual encounter since that unfortunate pairing in college. A residual shudder rippled across her flesh. She'd never get *that* drunk again no matter how many centuries she wandered through. Lifting her gaze to Maxwell's amused expression; she waved the candlestick across the bed. "Well? Answer me. Did we have sex or not?"

Maxwell rumbled with another deep chuckle. "*Not,* lass." He pulled himself up straighter in the chair. "I'd never foist myself on a helpless woman. 'Twould be a truly dishonorable thing to do...taking advantage of a maid who is not in control of her body? Ye insult me with such a question."

Trish wilted back against the pillows and stretched out her legs. Remembering Maxwell's words, she straightened again and shook the candelabra in his face. "So, what the hell were you going to say about two bodies are? Are what? Finish it!" She'd never met such an infuriating man in all her life. Too bad he'd saved her life because if he didn't stop teasing her with half-explanations, she was going to be forced to kill him.

A teasing grin peeped out from beneath Maxwell's mustache, curving his full lips to the side. "Ye didna give me time to finish what I was about to say. When two souls intertwine, the flesh of the bodies becomes exhausted with the joining. To seal the binding of the souls, the two must touch while they rejuvenate together. Two beings traveling the realm of sleep in a pairing is one of the most unifying acts for joined souls since the dawn of man."

They'd slept together. *Really slept.* Trish eased out a relieved sigh. *Good.* Nothing else had happened. *Perfect.* Trish squirmed among the pillows. If she hadn't wanted anything to happen, why did she suddenly have a vague feeling of disappointment?

Maxwell pushed himself up from the chair and stretched again, raising his long arms toward the ceiling. "Now that we've settled that, what say ye to getting a bit more sleep?"

Trish stared at him; disbelief dropped her chin to her chest. Was he seriously thinking about climbing back into bed with her? Naked? She had two words for the man: *Hell. No.* Trish tossed the metal candlestick to the floor with a resounding *thunk.* Waving a hand toward the door, she slid down into the covers. "You can sleep all you want. Out there. Somewhere. In another room."

"But—"

"But nothing." Trish rolled over on her side with her back toward Maxwell. "You said you wouldn't *foist* yourself where you weren't wanted."

"Lass—"

Pulling the covers up around her ears, Trish shook her head down deeper into the pillow. "Find another place to sleep, Maxwell. Go foist yourself somewhere else."

EIGHT

Trish centered the door facing between her shoulder blades, leaned hard against the wooden beam and slid her body up and down. *Damn.* She hated wool. Even with a linen tunic between her skin and the borrowed dress, the heavy weave scratched her skin like a branch of stinging nettles. Trish didn't care what Ciara advised. As soon as she figured out where they'd stashed them, she was switching back into her own clothes.

Giving up on the useless rubbing, Trish grabbed the neckline of the dress and yanked it back up into place. The dress's previous owner must've been at least two sizes bigger because there was plenty of room to spare. She smoothed her hands along the darted seams running down the sides. Trish frowned, noticing the unusually small circumference of her waist. She must've lost a few pounds while she'd been out of commission. Peeping inside the front of the gown, Trish shook her head. Yep. The girls had definitely shrunk at least a full cup size. The boobs were always the first to go.

Her stomach growled as the warm yeasty fragrance of baking bread wafted under her nose. Trish sniffed in an approving lungful of the mouth-watering scent, swallowing hard against her empty belly flooding her taste buds with anticipation. She was starving. Maybe if she followed her nose, she'd score a buttered crust of the delicious stuff.

Trish trailed her hands against the pale gray wall of the hallway, concentrating on maintaining her balance. Her stomach growled a louder protest as a fresh wave of savory aromas floated through the air. Pressing a hand against her gurgling waist, Trish curled her toes in the soft doeskin slippers as a brief wave of dizziness stopped her in her tracks. The roughly woven carpet centered on the floor didn't look like it would be a very adequate cushion for a fall. Trish leaned against the wall and closed her eyes until the spinning sensation passed. She wasn't about to bust her butt in the hallway on her first foray out of her room. She inhaled deeply through her nose and blew out short, controlled bursts from between tightly pursed lips. "I can do this. I'm just a little weak. I've just got to get my land legs."

"What the hell are ye doin', woman? Are ye tryin' to end up back in the sickbed?"

Trish jumped at the sound of the booming voice and flattened her back against the wall. Maxwell. She should've known. He'd been a bit bossy ever since she'd ousted him from her room when she'd first regained her health. Bracing her hands against the stone blocks at her back, she bit back one of her favorite expletives and opted for good old sarcasm instead. "So, you think startling the living crap out of me is going to help matters?"

Maxwell's scowl deepened; his bushy eyebrows knotted tighter over an irritated gaze. "Ciara said ye wished to join the family downstairs. She also said she told ye I'd be up here soon to fetch ye and help ye navigate the staircase. Ye're still a bit weak and ye don't know yer way around the keep. Do ye never listen to what's best for ye?"

Trish flattened her palms tighter against the grainy surface of the wall and steadied her balance by shifting her feet a few more inches apart. "I believe I know what's better for me than anyone else around here." Irritation fueled more adrenaline in her veins, flushing her skin with prickly heat. "And I know my way around this keep as well as you do. Back in my time, I usually stay here about five months out of the year." Lordy, she wished she'd found her clothes. This wool was eating her alive. Trish slid one hand up the bell-shaped sleeve of the other arm and scratched as high as she could reach.

Maxwell glared at her, thumbs hooked in the wide black belt around his waist and feet spread as though he were about to tackle any entity happening along. He didn't say a word, just narrowed his eyes into a fierce stare and slightly tilted his head.

"Don't stand there glaring at me like that. That look might scare children but it doesn't faze me in the least." Trish yanked her sleeve back into place, pushed away from the wall, and turned to walk away. The red weave of the carpeting centered in the hallway heaved up like a rolling wave, undulating back and forth in her field of vision with a nauseating spin. Trish slapped a hand across her mouth and swallowed hard against the rising bile burning at the back of her throat. She staggered sideways. The walls spun faster and dodged away from her extended hand. Trish closed her eyes as a pair of rock-hard arms circled about her shoulders and scooped behind her knees to pull her against a warm firm chest.

"Ye've not eaten in days, woman. Ye're weak as a newborn calf." Maxwell settled Trish more comfortably against his body, his voice lowering to a gentler scold as he leveled his gaze with hers. "And ye're a damn sight too stubborn for yer own well-being."

The steady beat of Maxwell's strong pulse thumped through the scratchy folds of wool and warmed Trish's flesh. *Safety. Possessiveness. Caring.* Claiming traits intuitively transmitted into her awareness with every beat of Maxwell's heart. Trish shivered against the mesmerizing comfort she felt while cocooned in Maxwell's arms. What the hell was wrong with her? He was just a hard-headed man. Trish squirmed against his broad chest. "I'm fine. Put me down. My head started swimming a bit because I turned too fast."

Maxwell's warm breath caressed her cheek as his arms tightened their hold. His full lips flattened into a determined line beneath the curls of his reddish mustache as he swung into a long-legged stride.

Trish wiggled again and poked his shoulder, struggling against the annoying urge to relinquish the fight and snuggle deeper into his arms. "I said you could put me down. I'm not dizzy anymore. I can take it from here."

Silence. Maxwell stared straight ahead, swinging Trish back and forth in his arms with the rolling rhythm of his gait.

"Are you ignoring me?" Trish poked him again.

Maxwell's bottom lip twitched but he still didn't say a word. He just hitched her higher against his chest and sidled sideways down the curving staircase.

"Latharn was right. You are an insufferable asshole." Trish yanked her arms into an irritated cross over her chest. One way or another, she'd show Maxwell Sullivan that fifteenth-century behavior toward women wasn't going to work with her. "And I'm gonna tell Ramsay that his father described you perfectly."

Maxwell's bottom lip twitched again, as did the corner of his right eye. Trish couldn't tell if the man was about to growl or burst into booms of laughter. "Would you please do me the courtesy of responding?"

A quiet chuckle rumbled up from Maxwell's chest. "Sorry, lass. I guess ye could say I was lost in my thoughts."

"Lost in your thoughts?" Trish huffed. *Damn him.* How the hell could he be lost in his thoughts while lugging her down an endless flight of steps? Trish shifted her shoulders against the hardened muscles cradling her body. *Damn him straight to hell!* The more Maxwell pissed her off, the worse the infernal wool irritated her skin. She couldn't decide which was worse: burning with fury or prickling from the attack of the flesh-eating wool. "Well since I'm apparently too boring to hold your attention, would you mind telling me what you were thinking?"

One corner of Maxwell's mouth trembled beneath the shadow of his mustache as he paused on the first landing of the curved staircase. "I was just remembering a mare I once had. Ye are quite a bit like her."

She reminded him of a horse? Trish clawed at the itching skin burning at the back of her neck. If he ever set her down, she was going to kill him—*after* she stripped off the torturous dress setting her skin on fire. "And how, pray tell, do I remind you of a mare you once owned?"

Maxwell's face finally split into a blinding smile as he settled Trish on the carved wooden bench waiting at the bottom of the stairs. "My sweet little mare was quite the beauty. All who saw her loved her. But ye'd best take care when drawing close to her stall or ye would discover the viciousness of her bite."

The viciousness of her bite? Trish clenched her teeth with an irritated grind, as she rubbed her itching back against the jagged carvings of the bench. She'd show him *bite*. "You're quite the charmer, Maxwell. No wonder your sweet little mare tried to bite you. Whatever happened to her?"

Maxwell grinned and before Trish realized what he was doing, slid his hand down the back of her dress and scratched the elusive burning itch prickling just out of reach between her shoulder blades. The very itch she'd been dying to scratch ever since donning the cursed dress.

Oh lord have mercy. Please don't stop. Trish shivered and without thinking, flexed her back and turned into Maxwell's hand. "Lower and more to the right."

Maxwell's grin stretched wider but he complied, treating her burning flesh to the heavenly relief of a well directed scratch. "Aye. Yer just like my little mare. Ye're both divine sweetness and fully tamed as long as ye're scratched in all the right places."

Trish released an ecstatic shudder. Leaning forward, she braced her hands on her knees and shifted her body into his magical fingers like a cat directing its master's caress. "Less talk and more scratching. Every time you open your mouth, all you do is piss me off."

Maxwell's deep laughter exploded through the halls of the keep. Tucking his chin with a single nod, his eyes sparkled with amusement as he angled closer and adjusted the direction of his satisfying touch. "As ye wish, my little mare. As ye wish."

CHAPTER
NINE

Maxwell scanned the winding paths trailing about the private gardens. Thank the gods no one appeared to be about. He returned his gaze to Trish's shapely derriere, seductively swinging from side to side in her revealing pair of close fitting trews.

God's beard. Maxwell scrubbed his face with one hand, ending the motion with an absent-minded pulling of hair on his chin. Did all the women of Trish's time walk about in such revealing clothes? *Lore a'mighty.* From the back, the skintight clothing showed the cleft of her buttocks and the view of the front hinted at the treasures waiting to be enjoyed.

Maxwell adjusted his swollen member to a less obvious fold of his kilt and prayed for a sudden blast of cold Highland wind to give him some relief. Perhaps he'd best remain outside even after Trish decided to go in for supper.

Trish's laughter rang out as she lobbed an odd-shaped ball across the garden to Ramsay.

Maxwell grinned as he eased closer, taking care to move down an alternate path shielded by a row of carefully planted firs. The young trees barely reached his chin, the perfect height to observe Trish while she took in a little fresh air and played with the boys.

Maxwell chuckled at how Ramsay and Keagan took right to the lumpy ball Trish had fashioned from scraps of leather. What was the word she'd used to describe the knobby orb? *Base ball?* Aye...that was it. Maxwell moved soundlessly closer to the trio, biting back the urge to laugh as Ramsay spewed a Gaelic curse word as the ball flew past his head.

"Ramsay?" Trish shook a finger at the red cheeked lad. "I'm not positive about what you just said but I'm pretty sure you're not supposed to use that word."

Ramsay ducked his head as he turned to run for the ball but not before shooting a mischievous wink to Keagan.

"I saw that, Ramsay," Trish warned as she pulled her collar closer about her neck.

Maxwell edged his way through an opening in the firs and stepped out into the clearing. "The wind grows colder. Do ye no' think ye'd best be coming inside?"

Trish squeaked and jumped aside, one hand pressed against her throat. "Will you please stop sneaking up on me?" Waving a hand toward the two boys at the other end of the clearing, she shook her head. "And no, we're not ready to come inside. We've only been tossing around the ball for a little while. If you're cold, go on in. I know the way back to the kitchens."

Maxwell snorted, squared his shoulders and turned into the wind. "I'm no' cold. I'm a Highlander, lass. I find the bite of the breeze refreshing." And thank the gods for the chilly air cooling the stubborn member between his legs, or else he'd ne'er be able to walk. Maxwell shifted his stance and forced himself to keep his gaze fixed on Trish's face. "The color's high upon your cheeks and your wee fingers are red with the cold. It's no' been that long since ye were unwell. Ye need to take care."

Trish sniffed against the cold and pulled her sleeves down

farther over her hands. "My fingers are a bit numb with the cold. I wish my gloves had followed me down the rabbit hole."

"Rabbit hole?"

"Never mind." Trish grinned with a shake of her head.

Maxwell caught the ball, scowling at Keagan for lobbing it toward his head. Rubbing a thumb over the rough seams of the leather orb, Maxwell grinned at the uneven stitches. "I hope the stitches on your clothes are better than these else they'll never last."

Trish caught the corner of her lip between her teeth and hugged Ramsay to her when he ran to her side. "I don't sew my own clothing. I buy it. Ready-made. In a shop."

"Yep." Ramsay bobbed his head up and down in complete agreement. "Her and Mama buy a lot a stuff online too."

"Online?" Maxwell frowned. What the hell was *online*? Sometimes Trish and the boy said the oddest things. The future must be quite different.

"Yeah. Ye know. Online with computers and stuff." Ramsay pulled out from under the curve of Trish's arm and motioned out the shape of a box in the air.

Trish took the ball out of Maxwell's grasp and shoved it into Ramsay's hands. "Enough, Ramsay. Remember what we talked about. Why don't you and Keagan play a little more ball and then it's back to work."

Ramsay's smile disappeared and he tucked his chin against his chest. "Yes, ma'am."

As Ramsay scampered away to join his cousin, Maxwell searched Trish's face. "What did ye mean when ye told the boy to remember what ye'd said? He didna say anything amiss." An uneasiness stirred in Maxwell's gut. Secrets were rarely ever good.

Trish shrugged as she shuffled her feet in the thin layer of snow coating the flagstones of the path. "Ramsay and I have to be careful while we're here. It could be dangerous if we changed the past."

"How?" Trish's suddenly wary tone stirred Maxwell's already growing sense of uneasiness. "What do ye fear, Trish? Ye must know that none of us would ever allow anything to harm either you or the boy."

"I know." Trish edged a few steps back and worried a hand through the longer length of her unruly curls. "It's one of those things that's hard to explain." Trish paused, frowning as she struggled to continue. "It's like the perpetual riddle: if I go back in time and accidentally kill my father before he meets my mother, how will I be born to go back in time to accidentally kill my father?"

"God's beard, woman. What the hell kind of madness is that?" Maxwell sucked in a lungful of the icy winter breeze. Surely, the cold air would clear the confusion from his head.

"Think about it. It makes my point." Trish tucked her hands up into her armpits and squinted against the rising wind peppered with bits of snow. "Ramsay and I have to be extremely careful about anything we say or do while we're here in the past. The consequences of our actions could be disastrous."

While they're here in the past. An unfamiliar weight pulled against the corners of Maxwell's heart. Trish and the boy didn't plan on staying. Maxwell ran his tongue across the base of his mustache, licking away the melting snowflakes trapped in the hair. Why the hell did it bother him so much? The fact that they might go away? "When do ye plan on leaving? You and the boy."

Trish brought her reddened hands up to her face, cupped them together over her mouth, and blew out a steamy breath. Rubbing them together, she raised her shoulders in the faintest shrug and stared down at the ground. "I don't know when we'll be able to leave. Ramsay's got to figure out how to get us back since it was kind of an accident that we ended us here in the first place."

"I see." Well no. He really didn't see. He'd just begun to grow accustomed to the fact that the keep seemed a much more interesting place with the addition of the fiery redhead. Maxwell unwound his plaid from about his shoulders and wrapped it around Trish. "I know ye canna stand wool but the cold grows stronger and that bit of cloth ye've got around yer body will do no good against the storm." Maxwell paused; his face close to Trish's hair as he tightened the cloth around her shoulders. *Damn.* But the woman smelled fine. She had an alluring sweetness about her, like the spices Ciara used in the treats she fashioned during Yule. Trish's wild curls blew against his skin. Maxwell closed his eyes, forcing himself not to bury his face in the silk of Trish's tousled hair.

"Thanks, Maxwell." Trish cleared her throat and eased a step back.

Maxwell opened his eyes; his gaze centered on Trish's flushed cheeks and nervously shifting eyes. Trish wouldn't meet his gaze. Her focus darted everywhere except for Maxwell's face. Surely, she could feel it too. It couldna be just him.

Maxwell reached out, cupping her chilled face in the palm of his hand; his thumb caressed the velvet of her cheek. He had to know. Steeling himself, Maxwell leaned in and bent his head to hers. With the barest touch, he tasted her mouth, sampled the softness of her lips. Relief flooded through him as the weight of her hand eased up the side of his neck and pulled him closer still. Aye. She felt it too.

Maxwell cradled her closer, deepened the kiss and reveled in the warm sweetness of her mouth. She opened to him, welcomed him in and gave back in return.

Mine. The strength of the word surged through Maxwell's being. *Mine and no other's.* Maxwell deepened the claiming, cradling her head in the crook of his arm as he pulled her body tight against his. He traced his fingers along the warmth of her throat and tickled them up into the softness of her hair. *Lore a'mighty.* Trish tasted sweeter than he'd imagined. What the hell were they doing standing in the middle of a frozen garden when they could be enjoying each other in the comfort of his soft warm bed?

"Come with me," he whispered against her mouth. "I need ye more than ye know."

Trish turned her head slightly away, her hand sliding from around his neck to rest in the center of his chest. Her voice fell to such a soft whisper, Maxwell strained to hear her words. "I shouldn't, Maxwell. It wouldn't be right." Her tiny hand pressed against his breastbone, then slowly slid away. "As soon as Ramsay figures out a way, we'll be returning to our time."

Maxwell slid a finger beneath her chin and raised her face to his. "Ye could find happiness here, Trish. This ripple of time is no' all that bad."

Trish shook her head and stepped away. "No." She pulled Maxwell's plaid tighter about her shoulders and turned toward the outer archways of the keep. "I don't belong here, Maxwell. I've got a life back in my own time. As soon as I can figure out a way, I'm going to return to it."

Maxwell clasped his hands behind his back, watching Trish's swaddled form follow the wandering path out of the garden. Realization twisted through his heart, chilling him more than the frigid wind. Trish had to stay. She didn't belong in the far-off future. Trish belonged with him.

CHAPTER
TEN

Deodorant. Tampons. Toothpaste. Steaming hot showers. Grape soda. And ice cream. What she wouldn't give for a humongous bowl of tongue-tingling butter pecan ice cream. Which item did she miss the most from the future? Hard to say. Probably a three-way tie between tampons, the shower, and ice cream.

Leaning forward on the window ledge, she gave herself to the velvety blackness of the starless sky. She caught her breath, a sudden feeling of claustrophobia wrapped around her and squeezed. The black of the night reached out like an endless, suffocating blanket. Strange how dark the night seemed when there wasn't any sort of manmade lighting piercing through its folds.

A resounding thud of a dropped book and a muffled curse interrupted the quiet of the room.

"I take that to mean that the spell wasn't in that book after all?" Trish didn't bother pulling her gaze from the bleak wintry night. She supposed she should scold Ramsay for his choice of words, but why bother? The boy was frustrated and she didn't really blame him. They'd been trapped in the past now for almost three months.

Any hope of returning to the future was wearing thin around the edges.

Trish closed her eyes and counted backward. Ramsay's little sister should've been born by now. In fact, as best she could calculate, the newest addition to the MacKay brood should be almost one month old. Trish turned, studying Ramsay's bent head shining auburn in the lamplight. Poor Latharn and Nessa. They must be heartsick and completely frustrated at the loss of their eldest son.

Ramsay lifted his head and wiped the back of his hand across his eyes. A lone teardrop escaped down the curve of his flushed cheek. Trish's heart ached. What consolation could she offer the boy? Tamping down the urge to gather Ramsay into her arms, Trish forced herself to remain sitting in the window seat. So helpless. She was the adult and what had she done to see them safely home? Nothing. A sense of failure festered in the pit of her stomach and soured on her tongue. "I'm sorry, Ram."

Ramsay cleared his throat, his voice quivering when he finally spoke. "I miss Ma and Da, Auntie Trish. Do ye think maybe they miss me just a little too?"

"Of course, they do." She couldn't resist him any longer. Trish rose from the pillowed bench stretched in front of the window and hurried to Ramsay's side. Wrapping an arm around his scrawny shoulders, she hugged him tight against her. "You know your mom and dad miss you just as much as you miss them. And I'm sure your brothers and your cousins are sad that you're gone as well."

"I bet Hamish isn't sad. I bet he's already laid claim to all my stuff." Ramsay leaned forward over the table, propping his chin atop his folded arms.

"Now Ram." Trish swallowed a giggle. Knowing the avaricious Hamish, Ramsay was probably right. "You know your mom and dad aren't going to let anyone pillage your stuff."

"Auntie Trish?" Ramsay whispered, his gaze focused on the flickering flames of the iron candelabra centered on the table.

"Yes, Ram?"

"What if it takes us years to get back? What if we canna get back at all?"

Trish's heart lurched. She couldn't tell the boy she feared the exact same thing. Ramsay needed to feel that she believed in him. Neither one of them could afford believing they'd never make their way back to where they belonged. "We'll get back. You've got to believe that or your magic won't work. You know that, Ram."

Ramsay sniffed, continuing to focus on the dancing yellow flame. "Yeah. But if we do make it back, then you won't get to see Maxwell no more. Won't that make you sad?"

Maxwell. Trish hugged herself and turned away from the boy. When had Ramsay gotten so perceptive? "Of course, I'd miss him but we don't belong here. Don't you remember all those lessons your father taught you about throwing the continuum out of balance?"

"The MacKays have always kept the continuum thrown upon its ear. Why should any of that change now?"

Trish whirled toward the doorway and the mesmerizing sound of the deep baritone voice that always filled her with conflicting emotions. Nodding toward the smiling boy at the table, Trish pointed toward the door. "Ramsay, why don't you go see if Keagan's had any luck translating those scrolls he keeps in his room?"

Ramsay winked at Maxwell then hopped up from the table and bounced toward the hall. "Sure, Auntie Trish. I'll check with Keagan and I'll prolly spend the whole entire night in his room. So's you can have some time to yourself."

Trish decided against scolding Ramsay when she noticed the look on Maxwell's face. As the patter of Ramsay's footsteps faded to nothing, she leveled an accusing gaze on Maxwell. "Did you put him up to that little statement?"

Maxwell raised both hands level with his shoulders, his mustache quivering as he obviously struggled not to smile. "I've not seen the lad all day. He's been up here with you."

"Why do I not believe you?" Trish edged farther away from the blazing hearth. The room suddenly seemed overly warm.

Maxwell closed the door and leaned against it. Trish heard the metallic clink of the latch as he slid the bolt into place.

"Why are you locking me in?" As Maxwell moved toward her, a wave of molten heat centered in Trish's belly and spread to regions much lower.

Maxwell shook his head ever so slightly and pulled her into his arms. "I'm no' locking ye in, sweetling. I'm bolting the rest of the world out." He bent his head and tasted her with a hesitant kiss, gently suckling her bottom lip into the inviting warmth of his mouth.

Trish groaned, leaning into him as she tangled her fingers into the hair at the base of his neck. A hint of ale laced his delicious flavor as she opened to his exploring tongue. His hands slid down her back, cupped her buttocks, and pulled her into his hardness. Trish shivered, pressing tighter until his heartbeat hammered between her breasts. She needed this, needed him. Damn, she'd wanted this so long.

"Tonight." His voice rasped hoarse with urgent need; his warm breath tickled down her throat. "I canna wait any longer."

All the reasons why she shouldn't whirled through Trish's mind. 7All the reasons why she should pulsed liquid heat between her thighs. "To hell with it." Trish gasped against the delicious assault of his lips across her collarbone. "I've never behaved myself this long before." She slid a hand up Maxwell's muscled thigh, groaning with a satisfied shudder as she confirmed what a true Highlander wore beneath his kilt.

Maxwell scooped her up and took her over to the table, gently laying her atop the sturdy oak. He trailed his fingers down along her throat, pausing with a teasing touch when he reached the sensitive skin between her breasts. "If ye'd worn your dress like a proper woman, I'd have a much easier time getting to your charms."

Trish unzipped her jeans, slid them down her hips and popped open the snaps of her blouse. Licking her lips, she reveled in the shocked delight shining in the depths of Maxwell's gaze. "If I were a proper woman, I doubt very much that I'd be spread across this table like your own personal banquet."

"Now there's a fine idea, if I do say so myself." Maxwell slid his hands under her hips and stepped between her thighs. With slow deliberation, he ran the tip of his warm wet tongue in maddening circles along the flesh of her inner thigh.

Trish closed her eyes, arching her back and writhing beneath the delicious tickle tracing up her leg. "Dammit, Maxwell. You're killing me. Please..."

"Please what?" Maxwell paused, blowing a long hot breath into the center of the reddish curls directing him to the prize.

Trish panted and gripped the sides of the table. Hooking her legs atop his shoulders, she pulled, urging him forward. "Please... Maxwell...I need you."

"Do ye now?" Maxwell chuckled, dipping his tongue into her pulsating center. "Mmm..." Maxwell purred as he dove deeper and suckled her aching nub. "Sweeter than honey-flavored wine."

Trish shuddered, filled her hands with his thick hair, and pulled his mouth harder into her body. *Lord have mercy but this man knows how to use that tongue.* Arching her back, Trish shook with the need coursing through her flesh. A purring groan tore from her throat as thrumming pleasure threatened imminent explosion. When Maxwell treated her to a slow luscious finger buried deep and suckled hard on her nub, Trish released a shouted, *"Yes!"* Shudders of uncontrollable ecstasy shook her as delight reached critical mass and pushed her over the edge. Wondrous spasms rippled through her as she clenched Maxwell between her legs. Moaning, she laced her fingers in his hair and rocked into his talented mouth with gyrating hips.

"Take me, Maxwell. Take me now," she gasped without opening her eyes. Damn, she needed to feel him pound inside her. She needed...more.

"Aye, m'love." Maxwell raised his head and pulled her down to the edge of the table. "'Tis definitely time for the claiming."

A satisfied growl escaped from Maxwell's lips as he slid partially into her depths. Trish wrapped her legs around his waist, gasping as he paused. "Don't stop now, for heaven's sake."

"I dinna want to hurt ye, love." Maxwell's face reddened as he struggled with self-control. "God's beard, woman, hold still. Ye are so damn tight ye are gonna make me spill my seed before I've given ye any pleasure."

"If you give me any more pleasure, I'm gonna freakin' die." Trish dug her nails into the knotted muscles of Maxwell's forearms locked on either side of her body. Wriggling her hips, she clenched him tighter with her legs, pulling him deeper into her body. "Enough talk. Dive in and move!"

"Ye are a bossy wench." Maxwell groaned as he buried himself into her depths. Sliding back out, he immediately hammered back into her and pressed his forehead against hers. With a quick kiss to the end of her nose, Maxwell repositioned his hands closer to her hips. "But who am I to argue with a woman who knows what she wants?"

And then he pounded into her until their cries melded as one and echoed into the night.

CHAPTER
ELEVEN

"She'll no' be traveling back now. Ramsay shall return to his family alone." Maxwell drained the tankard in one long draught, then lowered his mug with a triumphant thud to the table.

Faolan leaned forward, eyes round as he tapped a finger against Maxwell's forearm. "She agreed to stay here—in this time? Ye asked her to complete the melding and become your wife?"

Maxwell brushed away Faolan's hand as he pushed himself up from the table. "I dinna have to ask her to be my wife. She should know that I'll no' have any son of mine growing up in the future without a father."

"A son?" Faolan halted amid rising from his seat, spreading both hands atop the table as though he'd suddenly grown very weak. "Are ye sayin' Trish carries your child?"

Why did the man sound so surprised? Did he think only a MacKay was capable of siring bairns in just one bout of pleasure? Maxwell paced across the rush-covered floor, scattered reeds greeting every step with a dry shooshing crunch. "She could be with child. 'Tis too soon to know for certain." Maxwell waved a hand through the air. "But I'm certain my son took hold last night. 'Twas *different* than I've ever experienced before."

"It was different because you're in love with Trish, you pompous idiot." Ciara swept in from the archway connecting the dining hall to the main kitchen, her dark eyes snapping with indignation. "And don't you think you need to talk with Trish before you decide her future?" Ciara jabbed an accusing finger mere inches from her husband's nose. "Men! What the hell is wrong with the lot of you?"

Faolan backed away, hands held high as though that would help deflect Ciara's words. "What the hell did I do, wife? 'Tis Maxwell who's acting the fool."

"Well, I will truly be damned." Maxwell spun away from the soothing heat of the roaring hearth and stormed back toward the table. "God's beard, man. Where's your loyalty?"

"With my wife. I tend to value my hide." A mischievous grin played across Faolan's lips as he took a swat at Ciara's rump then jumped back when she snapped the twisted linen dangerously close to his most prized appendage. Rubbing a hand against the front of his kilt, he hitched a bit farther out of her reach. "Mercy, woman. Mind your aim. Ye nearly stung me bollocks."

"Next time I will." Ciara stretched the rag between her hands, wrapping the ends tighter around her knuckles and snapping it as taut as a bowstring. "And you—"

Maxwell retreated a few steps behind the safety of the broad trestle table. He'd be damned if he'd stand there and be unmanned with a kitchen dishrag before having a chance to defend himself. "I meant no disrespect to Trish. I just know she feels the same." How could she not? His traitorous cock stiffened at the mere mention of her name. The memory of last night's sweet love play raged anew through his flesh.

"I feel the same about what?" Trish emerged from the entry hall, tucking a cream-colored tunic inside the loose waistband of an unusual skirt colored with what looked to be every shade of a faded, weary rainbow.

"What in Brid's name are ye wearing?" Maxwell circled Trish, stroking his fingers through the wiry hair of his beard as he peered closer at the odd-looking weave. If he didn't know better, he'd swear she'd wrapped one of the tapestries from the second floor around her body.

Two patches of red blazed high on Trish's cheeks, highlighting the splash of freckles peppered across the bridge of her nose. Her chin lifted a bit higher as she spun in a slow circle. "You know I can't wear wool." She paused, smoothing a stubborn puckered seam running down the side of her hip. "Ciara sent for a hank of heavy linen but it's not here and my other clothes aren't dry from their latest scrubbing. So I kinda made this fashion statement out of one of the hangings in my room. It's silk or something." Trish paused and smoothed a hand across the top of her multi-colored thighs. "Whatever it is at least it doesn't make me itch."

Maxwell held his breath. If he laughed, she'd surely skin him alive. Tapping a finger against the tip of his nose, he hid an uncontrollable grin behind his hand. *Lord ha' mercy, but she is a fine one.* The stubborn lass cared more about comfort than the gossip she'd stir walking around in such unusual garb. Swallowing hard against the almost unbearable urge to chuckle, Maxwell tucked his chin against his chest and clasped his hands behind his back. "'Tis verra...fine. And I must say, 'tis much more proper than your trews from the future."

"Jeans, Maxwell." Trish rolled the over-long sleeves up higher on her slender arms. "They're blue jeans. Remember?"

"Aye." Maxwell nodded and offered his arm. Perhaps, now was the best time to sit the lass down and discuss how things should be between them.

"So, tell me." Trish slid an arm through his, treating his tensed muscles to the warm softness of her tempting full breast as she pressed close against him "What was everyone fussing about when I came into the room?"

"Beg pardon?" What the hell did the woman just say? Damned

if he couldn't concentrate when the fullness of her flesh and the sweetness of her scent rendered him incoherent. Maxwell helped her maneuver the broad bench beside the table, reluctantly letting go of her hand once she'd settled into place. "What was it ye said?"

"I said"—Trish patiently drew out the words as though speaking to a slow-witted servant—"what was everyone talking about? I thought I heard my name mentioned."

"Tell her, Maxwell." Ciara folded her arms across her chest, a wicked look of supreme smugness spreading across her face.

One of the kitchen lads scurried into the room, a pewter tray nearly as large as a good sized shield teetered on his shoulder.

"Oh good," Trish scooted closer to the table, stretching to see what the tray held. "I'm starving and do I detect the aroma of some of that lovely tea?" Rubbing her hands together, Trish wiggled in her seat like an excited child about to open a cherished gift. "I love the tea here."

The gangly lad grinned and bobbed his head in silent greeting while settling the teapot, a cup, and a platter of thick-sliced bread spread with a generous dollop of butter in front of Trish.

"Ye see?" Maxwell settled on the bench beside her, wrapping a possessive arm around her waist. "I told ye she'd be having my bairn."

Trish froze in the middle of sinking her teeth into the dark-brown bread. "What the hell did you just say?" she mouthed around the hunk of crust.

Maxwell reached for the pot and filled her cup with the steaming amber liquid. He'd better have her tea at the ready. Trish sounded as though she were about to choke. Sliding the cup directly in front of Trish, an uneasy feeling of impending doom shivered chill bumps across his flesh. "I said that I was probably right. After last night, ye could verra well be carrying my son."

Trish settled the thick slice of bread beside the cup on the table. Brushing the crumbs from her hands, she slowly lowered them into her lap. Her mouth flattened into a determined line, her jaw muscle twitching as though she gritted her teeth.

Maxwell swallowed hard. From the intensity of the red on the lass's cheeks, he'd bet his best horse that she was about to explode.

"I cannot believe—" Trish paused, eyes narrowing as she spit out the words in a slow irritated hiss. "I cannot believe," Trish repeated, her trembling hands knotting into balled up fists on either side of her cup. "I cannot believe you sat here this morning and told everyone what we did last night. Where in the *hell* is your sense of decency? I may not be the virginal sort but at least I don't traipse around advertising my escapades. Haven't you ever heard that old saying that a true gentleman never kisses and tells?"

Maxwell flinched. Trish's voice had an endearing way of accenting certain words depending on her current frame of mind. But by the way she'd just spiked the word *hell*, he'd really pissed her off. "Faolan and Ciara are family to me." Noting Ciara's triumphant glower, Maxwell waved a hand toward Faolan. "Well, Faolan is family to me. Ciara is more like punishment for my sins."

Ciara snorted and dismissed Maxwell's words with a flit of the knotted towel. "Don't be embarrassed, Trish. We'll ensure that anything discussed in this room—" She gave her husband a meaningful look before she settled onto the bench. *"Stays* in this room."

Maxwell risked resting a hand across Trish's clenched fist. "I am an honorable man, sweetling. I would never spout details of anything that should be kept between the two of us. I was merely pointing out to Faolan and Ciara that I would never abandon my child to the future and I was certain ye would feel the same." There. That sounded so much better. Surely, Trish would see the sense of it now. Maxwell shifted on the hard bench and waited for what seemed like an eternity. *God's teeth.* Why didn't the woman say something instead of sitting there with her hands knotted into fists?

Trish's gaze lowered as she slid her hands out from under Maxwell's and folded them in her lap. "I will still be going back to the future, Maxwell." The pink tip of her tongue swiped nervously across her lower lip. "And you don't have to worry about the possibility of your child growing up without a father." Inhaling a deep shaking breath, Trish raised her gaze and turned to face him. "I'm not able to have children."

An uncomfortable silence filled the room and stole the warmth from the air. Trish wrapped her hands around her steaming mug of tea and took a hesitant sip. Her gaze remained fixed on the amber liquid as she lowered the cup to the table. "Well, that was a conversation killer."

Maxwell stared at the flush of red creeping up Trish's creamy throat. She couldna have children? Barren? How? "How do ye know..." Maxwell struggled, both sympathy for Trish and frustration with not understanding vying for possession of his mind. "How do ye know ye canna have children? Have ye already tried?" There. He'd said it. He didn't truly want to think of Trish having children with anyone but himself but he had to be realistic. After last night, he knew for certain she hadn't been a virgin but he'd prefer not to know the intimate details of her past. "Trish?" he leaned closer and whispered her name when she remained silent.

"Didn't you notice my lovely scar the plastic surgeons weren't able to erase?" Trish refused to look Maxwell in the face. Instead, she leaned forward, forearms on the table, staring down into the mug she circled with her hands.

Maxwell glanced at Ciara, then Faolan, frowning when they both slightly shook their heads. What the hell was she talking about? A scar? "All I recall about your...um...body"—Maxwell shifted uncomfortably in his seat—"is the beauty I beheld."

An almost imperceptible smile quivered at one corner of Trish's mouth as she rhythmically smoothed her thumbs in circles against the sides of the mug. "Well." Trish bowed her head and cleared her throat. "It was pretty dark in the library last night."

"I think we'd best leave." Faolan pulled on Ciara's arm while rising from his chair.

Ciara pulled her elbow out of her husband's grasp, crossing both arms over her chest. "Only if Trish doesn't need us here. It's her decision. I will not have her thinking we'd desert her or that we do not care."

Trish finally raised her head, huffing a humorless laugh as she rubbed a trembling hand across her eyes. "You're more than welcome to stay. I feel as close to the two of you as I do Nessa and Latharn."

Ciara and Faolan exchanged troubled looks and settled back down at the table.

Maxwell smoothed his hand across the satin of the well rubbed wood of the table. If only he'd known. A knot tightened in the center of his chest. He wished he'd never broached the subject. "What are ye tryin' to tell me, Trish? Just come out and say it."

A deep sigh escaped Trish as she turned to face him. "Several years ago...when I was much younger and in college, a man attacked me."

Rage clouded Maxwell's vision with a red haze, pumping a burning thirst for vengeance through his body. He bit back the roar he longed to release. Instead, he jerked his head forward with a stiff nod. "Go on."

Trish tilted her head, closing her eyes as though she couldn't bear to see anyone's expression while she told her tale. "He forced me by knife point into an abandoned building, raped me, sliced me into a bloody pulp, and then planned on torturing me until I gave up and died."

"If I'd been there, I'd ha' killed the bastard...with the cruelest death possible." Maxwell forced the words out, his voice rasping with the sense of injustice screaming in his head. "I suppose the cur left ye for dead?"

Trish shook her head, tracing a finger around the rim of the cup as she sat straighter on the bench. "No. Nessa heard my screams. She saved my life by driving a spike through the back of his head with a well aimed piece of lumber." Releasing the mug, Trish flattened her hands atop the table, staring down at her fingers as she spoke. "She saved my life, but I'm afraid she didn't get there in time to save my body from a great deal of damage."

"I hope the bastard suffers a painful eternity searing deep in the bowels of hell."

"Me too, Maxwell." Trish finally met his gaze. "But that's why you don't have to worry about any children from me."

Maxwell scooped Trish's ice cold hand between his own, rubbing the tops of her knuckles with his thumb. "I wasna worried, my dear sweet lass. I was just saying that I'd never abandon ye to raise a bairn alone."

A pained expression tightened around Trish's mouth as she avoided Maxwell's gaze. She drew in a deep shuddering breath and stared down at their linked hands. "I have to return to the future. No matter what happened between us last night. I've got to go back to my life."

Maxwell settled Trish's hands down into her lap, hesitating for a brief moment while he stared at the top of her curly head. If only he could see inside her mind. Maybe then he could figure out why she was so dead set on returning to her time. *Dammit.* Releasing her hands, he rose from the bench. "Ye are mistaken, lass. Ye need to stay. Whether ye can bear any children or not, ye now belong here just as much as I do."

Trish raised her head and finally met his gaze. Maxwell couldn't bear the denial in her eyes, couldn't bear the determination in the tilt of her head. He rose from the bench and stormed from the room before Trish had a chance to reply.

CHAPTER

TWELVE

A deep voice, rhythmic with a patient sing-song cadence, murmured through the wide seams of the weathered door. Trish paused, a hand resting against the rough gray wood and listened with her head bowed. Her heart fluttered right before it sank like a weight to the pit of her stomach. She'd recognize those rumbled "r's" anywhere. Trish closed her eyes and fought against the quivering excitement Maxwell's voice always sent tingling through her. *Damn the man.* She'd never had this problem before. How had Maxwell seemingly connected—no, not connected—gained control? Yes. Gained control over every part of her so that even the sound of his voice sent her into a tailspin?

Easing back a step, she stared at the door, willing the ancient wood to provide all the answers. Was she ready for another confrontation with Maxwell? Could she possibly win? Trish pinched the bridge of her nose, massaging the burning corners of her weary eyes and tried to ignore the nagging voice in her head hissing out the truth. *No. I'll never win against Maxwell's insistence that I stay, because I really don't want to go.*

Trish pressed her palms against her temples then smoothed

shaking fingers through her errant curls. She couldn't handle another shouting match right now. She was too weary from helping Ramsay pore over all the spell books in the tower. And they'd found nothing. Trish massaged the tensed muscles at the back of her neck, wincing at the tenderness of the knots.

Maybe they should just give up. Hours of squinting at faded text by the golden light of the iron candelabra had only rewarded her with a stiff back, grainy eyes, and about an hour's worth of a head-bobbing doze. And they'd still come away empty-handed.

Irritation deepened the ache in the tensed muscles bunched at the back of her neck. If she didn't know better, she'd swear Ram was deliberately leading them down blind alleys. The boy had missed his parents terribly at first but with every month they'd been separated from the far-off future, he'd settled more comfortably in the current past.

"I know ye are there. Ye might as well come inside out of the weather. The spring rains will soak ye to the skin if ye stand long 'neath the eaves."

How had he known she stood on the other side of the door? Trish gnawed on the inside corner of her lip. Maybe if she ignored him and walked away, she could still escape.

"Ye canna run from your heart, lass. I never took ye for a coward."

Oh, he would throw down that gauntlet. Nobody called her a coward. Steeling herself against what she knew would soon elevate into another tirade, Trish pushed the door open. Might as well grab that stubborn Scottish bull by his horns. There was no escaping Maxwell now. "I wasn't running. I didn't hear Ramsay or Keagan inside so I decided to look somewhere else for the boys."

"Aye." Maxwell grinned sadly over the shining back of a chocolate-colored mare. "Whatever ye say, lass."

The shooshing sound of the oval brush Maxwell ran down the mare's coat echoed through the stillness of the barn, mesmerizing Trish with its soothing rhythm.

"Why would ye come to the barn looking for the lads when

they've spent most of the day in the tower w'ye?" Maxwell smoothed the brush down the horse's side with another slow even stroke. His smile disappeared as he looked up from the rich flank shining in the torchlight. "Let there be no lies between us, Trish. We both deserve better than that."

Trish stiffened, planting her feet in the softness of the straw-covered dirt floor. Damn him. Would Maxwell never give up? "I'm tired of fighting with you, Maxwell. Why can't we just be civil and have a nice conversation?"

Maxwell didn't answer, just pulled the leather loop of the brush from around his hand and hung it on the peg. Sidling his way around to the front of the stall, Maxwell gave the mare's neck an affectionate rub as he stepped around her.

Great. Now he'd decided to use the silent treatment, pouting like a spoiled child. Trish bit back the angry words as she gathered up the folds of her skirt and turned to leave the barn. If he wanted to be a petulant ass, he could be one by himself.

"So, ye'll not give me the chance to answer ye?"

Trish stopped, tightened her grip on the folds of her skirts, and glared straight ahead. "It depends on the answer."

The rustle of the straw scattered on the ground grew louder with the crunching rhythm of Maxwell's steps. Trish didn't have to turn to know Maxwell stood just behind her. The heat of him radiated around her body, surrounded her with his presence. Trish swallowed hard. Her chilled flesh ached to melt into the warmth of his body, yearning to disappear into the comfort of his embrace. No. Never again. She could *not* allow that to happen.

Trish eased forward a bit, coming to an immediate halt as a strong hand wrapped around her upper arm and gently pulled in an attempt to turn her. Planting her feet, Trish fought against the urging of Maxwell's hand and also against the primal need screaming from the core of her flesh.

A warm rumbling chuckle shook through the stillness of the stable as Maxwell wrapped his arms around her waist and pulled her back against his chest. His wiry beard tickled against the side of her throat, triggering memories of other ticklish areas that Maxwell had teased with such an expert touch. She couldn't win against him. Trish closed her eyes, relaxed against him, and inhaled. Oil of cloves. Maxwell's scent always reminded her of that particularly fragrant spice.

He pressed his mouth against the back of her neck, tantalizing her skin with warm, wet flicks of his tongue. Maxwell nibbled a path to the tender spot behind her ear, pulling her tighter against his body as he suckled the lobe into his mouth.

Trish shuddered, hugging his arms tighter around her waist as she surrendered to the pleasures of his touch. *If only*...the words echoed from the corner of her mind not held prisoner by her need. "Dammit, Maxwell. Please stop." Trish pulled out of his embrace.

"As ye wish." Maxwell's quiet brogue was devoid of emotion.

"Maxwell, please..." Trish fought against the threat of tears. *Damnation.* Why had life become so complicated? She'd never had this much trouble shaking free of a man before.

"Which is it, lass?" Maxwell spread his feet farther apart and clasped his broad hands in front of his body. "As I see it, we must either move forward with these feelings or go our separate ways completely. If need be, I can leave MacKay keep today and return to my own home. I have no desire to be a mere acquaintance." He lifted his chin a notch and defiantly locked his jaw. "I will never be your friend."

"I never meant for any of this to happen." Trish cringed against the sound of her voice when it cracked at the end with a sob. Since when did she lose control? Since when did she not have the power to conquer any situation?

A sad smile pulled at the corner of Maxwell's mouth, barely hidden by his moustache. He shook his head and lowered his gaze to stare at the bare patch of ground between them. He shook his head slightly as his deep voice fell to just above a whisper. "Sometimes things happen because they were meant to be so. We're mere mortals, Trish. Sometimes we must trust where destiny takes us."

He made it sound so simple. Trust in the fates and fall into his arms, never questioning whether she risked harming mankind by altering the past. "I wish it were that easy." Trish closed her eyes, even her trembling excuse sounded defeated to her own ears.

"It is easy, lass. Ye need only ask yourself one question and then be honest with your answer." Maxwell paused, sucked in a deep breath then released it slowly between tensed lips. "Do ye feel the same connection I feel...or no'?"

Trish covered her face with trembling hands, pressing cold palms against her flaming cheeks. She knew the answer without even asking. She just couldn't bear to face it.

The silence between them took on a life of its own, growing to the size of a great hulking beast. Maxwell watched her with an unblinking stare, his gaze burning into her soul. Trish closed her eyes. She couldn't bear the emotions reflected in those eyes. They mirrored the feelings churning in her heart.

"How can I even attempt to do this?" The terrified whisper nearly caught in her throat. Trish forced it free with a hiccupping sob. "How do I–"

Maxwell closed the space between them with one quick lunge. Pulling her roughly into his embrace, he tilted her head back against his arm, forcing her to meet his gaze. "Ye will no' attempt to *do* anything, sweetling. Just choose a life at my side."

Trish swallowed hard and curled her fingers into Maxwell's wild shock of hair barely tamed by his warrior's braid. His heartbeat steady against her breasts, a silent promise to keep her safe. She could do this. The surety of his touch shattered any lingering doubts. To hell with the chaos of the twenty-first century; she belonged right here.

Snuggling her face into his chest, Trish closed her eyes as she released the last of her worries with a shuddering sigh. "I choose you," she whispered softly into Maxwell's tunic, wondering if she spoke loud enough for him to hear.

A deep rumbling laugh shook beneath her cheek, bubbled up from the depths of Maxwell's belly, and burst free to startle the horses in their stalls. Trish smiled and snuggled deeper into his strong embrace. Yep. Maxwell had heard her.

CHAPTER
THIRTEEN

"You'll speak your vows and then we'll light the fires of *Bealltainn.*"

"So, I take it there won't be a priest?" Trish turned into the brisk spring breeze caressing the face of the cliff and ran her fingertips across the rough surface of the glistening stone altar. Embedded bits of crystal danced like pinpoints of twinkling stars in the depths of the gray-black stone.

Ciara peeped around the side of one of the hulking obelisks standing butted upright against the massive rock table. "That won't be a problem, will it? I seem to be a bit more than most of the priests who wander through this area can handle."

Trish grinned at the mischievous glint in Ciara's eye. She had no doubt that the church might have a few problems accepting Ciara with her history as a former Fury and warrior-daughter of the goddesses Brid and Cerridwen. "No. The absence of a priest will not be a problem." An excited shiver rippled across her flesh triggering goose bumps atop her skin. She couldn't believe she had actually decided to stay in this time and become a Highlander's bride.

"You've chosen well." Ciara interrupted Trish's reverie with a soft pat atop her arm. "Maxwell is a good man."

Trish turned away from the chilling wind, tightening the fringed arisaid about her shoulders. "I just hope he doesn't regret choosing me." Staring down at the hard-packed earth surrounding the altar, Trish scrubbed a toe against a clump of newly sprouted greenery.

"I will never be able to give him children. Don't the men of this time feel an heir is pretty important?"

Ciara's dark eyes narrowed as she lifted her face to the fleeting rays of the springtime sun as it skittered beyond a bank of gray-white clouds. "Never underestimate the power of the time of *Bealltainn* or the whims and wishes of the goddess." Patting an escaped tendril of hair back into the dark shining knots of her intricate braid, Ciara faced Trish with a smile. "Leave the blessing of children to the Fates. All things happen for a reason, Trish. Whatever will be...will be, and Maxwell knows and accepts that."

Trish couldn't read the expression on Ciara's face and didn't really know if she wanted to. Sorting through her own chaotic emotions was enough of a chore without adding Ciara's cryptic messages to the list of things to decipher. Trish hugged herself and pulled the shawl tighter against the uneasy chill stealing across her flesh. No looking back. She had to keep telling herself that...and Ciara was right. Maxwell was a good man who had seemingly accepted all she'd told him whether it made him laugh or fume.

Another thought pulled at her heart, triggering an uncomfortable stab of guilt. Ramsay. The boy had said he wanted to stay in this time as well, said his family back in the twenty-first century would be just fine without him.

"He can stay here with us and grow up with Keagan. They're nearly the same age and an alliance with Ramsay will give Keagan an edge over the twins." Ciara's understanding smile tempered the fact that she'd read Trish's mind.

Trish walked to the edge of the cliff and gave herself to the breathtaking vista spread before her. But no matter how glorious the sparkling waves of the endless sea gleamed; she couldn't shake a sense of guilt from creeping into her heart. "Nessa and Latharn must be sick with worry. How could they not be? He is their son."

Ciara joined Trish alongside the cliff's edge, squinting her eyes against the endless wind. "I have sensed Latharn's power reaching across the web. Ease your heart, Trish. Latharn found his son here and knows the lad to be safe."

As the waves below crashed against the rocks with a steady rhythm, Trish watched the foam covered blue green peaks dance forward and then recede. "I know Nessa. Her heart is breaking because of the loss of her son, whether she knows he is safe or not."

A tern shrieked a forlorn cry into the wind as it floated white against the graying clouds. Trish tasted the brine of the sea kissing her lips as the spray sparkled like a handful of diamonds tossed to the winds. Swallowing hard, Trish sniffed against the sting of tears threatening to overflow. "I hope someday, she'll find it in her heart to forgive me for leading her son astray."

Ciara turned Trish away from the sea, urging her back down the timeworn path of barren earth surrounding the altar. "Now is not the time for regret or fretting over things you cannot change. Heartache is sometimes a necessary stone in the path of life, but you must not allow it to end your journey. The key to reaching the reward of your destiny is to keep moving forward."

Trish hugged Ciara's hand on her arm and took a deep breath. "I hope you're right, Ciara. I truly hope you're right."

CHAPTER

FOURTEEN

"And ye say Angus stands ready to play the pipes as soon as we light the fires?"

Faolan grinned and didn't bother to answer as he glanced out the stone archway, seated himself on the window's ledge, then turned to face Maxwell.

"Answer me, man! And wipe that wicked smirk off your face. What the hell do ye find so damn amusing?" Maxwell adjusted the straps of his finest sporran for what seemed like the fifth time. *God's teeth!* Why wouldn't the infernal thing hang where he wished? Running his fingers behind his tunic's tightly fastened collar, Maxwell yanked against the heavy linen, trying to loosen its hold on his throat. "And who in the hell told Sorcha to fashion this collar after a tightly knotted noose?"

Faolan scrubbed his hand across his freshly shaved face, an amused chuckle escaping through his fingers.

"Ye are a vile, wicked man, Faolan MacKay. A vile, wicked man." Maxwell stomped across the flagstones and joined Faolan at the window, stretching past him through the arch to peer up to the hill.

"It seems to me I remember havin' to shove your cowardly arse toward the altar on the day ye pledged to your bride."

Faolan clapped a hand to Maxwell's shoulder and pointed up the hillside toward the carefully constructed mound of broken limbs piled beside the stone altar. "Look just beyond the brush. See there? Angus awaits and he holds his pipes at the ready."

Maxwell exhaled, barely relaxing the strangle hold he held along the edge of the window's blocks. "This day will be the death of me. I ne'er thought I'd take a wife but now that I've met Trish, I canna stomach the thought of another day passing without her bearing my name."

"Ye'll be fine, old man." Faolan thudded him across the back once more as he rose from the windowsill. "Come. 'Tis time we joined your bride at the altar before ye fret yourself into an early grave."

As they stepped outside, Maxwell turned his face into the evening breeze, sucking in a great lungful of the crisp briny air. "'Tis a good evening to repeat our pledge. I feel Brid's blessing on the wind."

Faolan's smile faltered a bit as he matched Maxwell's ground-eating stride. "Aye, my friend. There is an energy crackling in the air. I feel it too."

Maxwell nodded to the throng of guests crowding the base of the hill. A comforting warmth filled his heart at the sight of so many smiling faces. "Thank ye, Faolan, and thanks to Clan MacKay for adding your blessings to this day."

Faolan nodded once as the crowd opened to the clearing holding the stone altar, revealing Trish waiting with Ciara. "Ye owe me no thanks, my friend. Now go and join your bride."

Reason fled him as Maxwell's gaze connected with Trish's beaming smile. His heart swelled at the sight of the Sullivan plaid draped about her shoulders. *Lore, the woman fills my soul with fire and wears my colors well.* Her shining curls blazed loose and free in the golden colors of the setting sun. Maxwell itched to bury his hands in the silky locks finally long enough to brush the tops of her shoulders.

As he stepped close to her side, he brought her trembling hand to his lips. "The sun rushes to hide behind the horizon 'cause it canna compete with your beauty."

The most delightful shade of rose he'd ever seen colored Trish's cheeks as she ducked her chin. She squeezed his fingers and leaned forward, so only he could hear her whisper. "Thank you...for everything."

Maxwell brought her clasped hands back to his lips again, lingering on the silky coolness pressed against his mouth. Words escaped him. *Lore.* He hoped the woman knew the joy filling his heart.

"Are you both ready?" Ciara stepped between the stone arches, her back to the glowing sun sinking into the ocean's glistening waves.

Maxwell glanced at Trish. Her shy nod and quivering smile warmed him like a dram of fine whisky. Cradling her hands between his own, he turned them both toward Ciara. "Aye. We are ready to pledge our lives and our souls."

Ciara stared at him, unblinking, her head tilted slightly forward.

Maxwell beamed back at her as he snugged Trish's hands against his chest.

Ciara cleared her throat, glanced down at Trish's hands then aimed a pointed gaze and an arched brow back at Maxwell's face. "Now, Maxwell," she finally whispered.

Realization hit Maxwell like a nudge in the ribs. It was time he revealed the ring. Freeing one hand and shoving it deep in his sporran, Maxwell gave Trish an apologetic smile as he searched the depths of the richly furred pouch. Where was the damn thing? He'd wrapped it carefully in a bit of soft hide to ensure it traveled well. A sense of relief flooded through him as his fingers touched the tightly wrapped bundle. Pulling the bit of yellowed hide from the pouch, Maxwell unwrapped the ring in the palm of his hand. Trish's sharp intake of breath assured him he'd done well.

The silver band gleamed with carefully polished knots and

whorls forming an intricate weave. A deep blue stone, an oval-shaped, sparkling sapphire nestled into the widest part of the band. Maxwell took Trish's shaking hand and seated the ring on her finger. Closing his hand over hers, he smiled into her eyes. "I canna imagine taking a breath without ye by my side. Ye own my heart and ye own my soul. I pledge all eternity to ye...my willful, beautiful bride."

A deafening roar exploded around them, plunging them into an inky darkness. Howling winds tore through them, shrieking through the upright stones of the altar. The pyres of gathered wood burst into flames, blazes shooting high into the air. Maxwell staggered back against the altar table; hands raised against the onslaught of debris stinging against his flesh.

"Trish," he roared into the gale, clawing against the blackness of the swirling cloud. A heart-wrenching scream reached him through the howling wind just before everything went black.

Icy raindrops plopped into his face as he rolled back against the base of the altar. The pelting drops shot faster from the clouds, melding into frigid sheets of water pummeling down the hillside. Maxwell squinted through the deluge, searching the gray, watery landscape for any sign of Trish. Crawling across the rain-slicked earth, he pulled himself to where Faolan and Ciara huddled in each other's arms.

"Where is she? Where is Trish? I canna see her," he roared to them, vying to be heard above the screaming storm.

Ciara shook her head and buried her face into Faolan's shoulder as he pulled her beneath the shelter of the stone altar's ledge.

"Tell me now!" Maxwell bellowed through the rain even though he feared the answer to his question.

Keagan shook his head as he elbow-crawled beneath the stone and crouched next to his mother and father. "They have gone back, Uncle Maxwell. They've both returned to their time."

CHAPTER

FIFTEEN

T he air swelled and then exploded between the stone pillars as though someone had squeezed the universe and popped that particular space like a delicate bubble. Drenched and shaking, Trish and Ramsay sprawled across the altar stone right where the universe spit them out.

"My baby!" Nessa rushed forward, pulling Ramsay into her arms and covering his closed eyes with kisses. "Ramsay, speak to me. Tell me you're all right. Please, Ramsay, say something."

"I'm okay, Mama," Ramsay croaked before going limp in her arms.

Trish closed her eyes. This could not be happening. Not this. Not now. Raking the back of her hand across her wet face, she strained to raise her head and force her eyes to focus. Latharn's concerned face swam into view. That was all it took. She collapsed back into an exhausted heap atop the stone, dragging a handful of the Sullivan tartan against her mouth to absorb her uncontrollable sobs. He was gone. She had returned to her time and lost the only man she'd ever attempted to love.

"Trish! Are ye hurt? Can ye speak?" Latharn eased a hand beneath her shoulders and carefully turned her toward him. "Trish. Why are ye weeping? Are ye no' glad to finally be home?"

Ramsay stirred in Nessa's arms, coughing and spitting as though he'd just been resuscitated after drowning. Unwinding himself from his mother's arms, he inched across the stone table and laid his cheek against Trish's arm. "Ye shouldha left Auntie Trish back there, Da. Ye yanked her away from her wedding day."

"Wedding day?" Nessa repeated in a horrified whisper. Pulling Ramsay back into her embrace, Nessa turned the boy's face to hers with a trembling finger under his chin. "What do you mean, Ramsay?"

"Auntie Trish loved Maxwell. Look at her hand. She wears his ring."

Trish curled her hand against her chest, cupping the precious ring against her heart. Rocking back and forth atop the altar, heart-wrenching sobs tore from her throat. Why couldn't Maxwell have returned with her instead of the damn ring? Blinded by a torrent of tears, Trish shoved her fingers into her waistband until she found the cold metal snuggled against her side. Working it free, she placed a man's silver ring on the stone beside her and covered it with a shaking hand. Ducking her head, she clenched her ringed hand to her chest and rocked back and forth, keening her pain to the wind. She hadn't given Maxwell his ring. Nor had a chance to repeat her vows.

"Send me back," she hissed through her tears into Latharn's startled face. "You've got to send me back right now. I'm in the middle of getting married."

A sorrowful shadow darkened Latharn's face as he slowly turned away. "I cannot, Trish. Please forgive me. I cannot reopen the portal."

"Bullshit!" Trish screamed, tripping over her long skirts as she scrambled off the altar stone. Stumbling forward, she fell atop Latharn's chest. Her clenched fists bounced against his body, fueled by her rage. "Don't stand there and lie to me. If you opened it once, you can do it again!"

She had to get back. Maxwell had to know that she really loved him. Panic ripped through her heart. She'd never said the words. She'd never told Maxwell she loved him. Balling up her fists, she swung at Latharn again, screaming as he locked his hands around her wrists and held her blows at bay. "Send me back to him now, dammit! I don't belong here anymore."

"I cannot!" Latharn hissed between clenched teeth. "Each MacKay chieftain is granted the magic to open the portal once during his lifetime. I used my chance to recover you and my son."

The painful truth hit Trish like a wall of ice water, knocking her to her knees. Ramsay was next in line to be laird and he'd used his one shot at the portal when he'd sent them back in time. Trish sucked in a shuddering sob as hopeless hysteria battered against the cruel logic unfurling in her mind. She would never see Maxwell again. She had used up her quota of MacKay chieftains. By the time Ramsay fathered an heir who could re-open the portal, a life with Maxwell would be a missed chance...like waking too soon from a lovely dream.

"Trish." Nessa's soft voice interrupted her misery and broke through the aching fog. "Even if you could go back, I don't think you would find what you expect."

Trish twisted the ends of the drenched arisaid tighter about her shoulders. A bone-chilling weariness settled into her flesh, making every movement a struggle. Not bothering to look up from the cold hard ground, Trish forced the words from her mouth. Even breathing took too much effort. What was the point really? "Cut to the chase, Nessa. I don't have the strength for your attempt to let me down gently."

A despondent sigh sounded from somewhere just above Trish's head, right before a pair of strong hands pulled her up to her feet. "Come on, Trish. There's something I think you need to see."

Somehow, her feet moved of their own accord as Nessa and Latharn pulled on her arms. Strange. How could a body continue to function and shift into auto-pilot when the heart and mind had been totally shattered? Trish shuffled forward, stumbling along the path as Nessa and Latharn led her down the hill.

"I know this will seem cruel but you need to know the truth. It would be pointless for you to return to the past, Trish. This is what you would find." Nessa pulled on Trish's arms, stopping them just inside the gate of the family cemetery. Her fingers dug into Trish's flesh, pointing her toward the corner of the headstone-filled garden. "Please don't hate me, Trish. But you've got to know that he is not there waiting for you. I'm so sorry but it's just too late."

Trish frowned at Nessa. What the hell was she babbling about? Of course, Maxwell would still be there waiting for her. Only a few moments had passed. If he wasn't here by her side, then he had to be back there standing beside that damn stone arch.

Nessa pulled her toward a taller headstone, slightly offset from the others. A dark foreboding squeezed icy claws around Trish's throat, threatening to cut off her air. "I don't need to see where he's buried, Nessa. Don't you think I've got enough sense to realize that if he didn't follow me to the future then he's long dead by now?"

Nessa's mouth tightened into a determined line and she pulled Trish closer to the stone. "You need to see *when* he died. It will help you move on...I hope."

Shrugging out of Nessa's grasp, Trish stomped over to the gravesite nestled in the corner. The name *Maxwell Sullivan* was carved deep and dark into the face of the soft gray stone. Trish stumbled forward, falling to her knees as she read the inscription that followed:

A day without the warmth of her smile...
...is an eternity spent in darkness.
Life is nothing without her.

Trish didn't understand how it could be possible. How could her heart hold so much pain and still beat within her chest? Below the inscription was the date. The numbers seemed to jump from the stone and slap her in the face. Trish hugged her body, rocking back and forth on the cold hard ground as tears blurred the engraving forever chiseled into her mind. Maxwell had given up. He had died the same day she had left.

CHAPTER
SIXTEEN

"Auntie Trish." Ramsay's hesitant call wafted through the garden like a sultry summer breeze.

"I'm here, Ramsay." Trish shifted positions on the stone bench, settling her chin in the crook of her arm propped atop the low stone wall. She had a clear view of his headstone from here —could just make out the words of the heart-breaking inscription. Perhaps it was silly but she always felt a bit closer to Maxwell whenever she sat here and watched over his grave.

"Mama says come to supper. Maitla's set the good table in the main hall and everyone's waitin' there for ye." Ramsay hitched back and forth along the stone path as though fearing his feet might take root if he stood too long in one place.

Without taking her eyes from Maxwell's headstone, Trish waved the boy away. "Tell your mama I'm not hungry. Tell everyone to go ahead and eat."

"Mama's gonna be mad," Ramsay replied in the age-old sing-song chant children always used to warn of impending parental rage.

Trish closed her eyes and took a deep breath, biting her tongue against the stinging retort she longed to hurl. She didn't give a damn if Nessa got mad. As a matter of fact, Trish didn't give a rat's ass about anything anymore. But it wouldn't be fair to take it out on Ramsay. After all, he was just a child. "If your mother gets mad, tell her..." Trish paused. No. She couldn't very well have the boy tell his mother to fight her own battles and stop hiding behind a child. "If your mother gets angry, she'll just get angry with me. It's no big deal, Ram. The world won't come to an end." Trish swallowed hard. No. The world wouldn't come to an end because it had already ended over a month ago when she'd lost the one she loved.

"I'm sorry, Auntie Trish." Ramsay coughed and shuffled a bit closer to rest his small hand atop her wrist. "I'm verra sorry for everything and I never meant to make ye so sad."

Trish pulled Ramsay into her lap and hugged him close. "I know you're a big boy and not fond of cuddling, but I need you to know how much I love you, Ram. And you need to know that you're not the one who made me sad. It's not your fault."

Ramsay sighed and settled against her chest, tucking his head beneath her chin. "I guess it's okay for ye to snuggle me just this once, Auntie Trish. 'Specially if it helps ye not be so sad."

Trish smiled and planted a kiss atop his head. "It helps, Ram. I promise it helps a lot."

"Would it also help if I held ye, lass?"

Trish froze, afraid to breath or move a muscle. Cripes almighty, she must be losing her mind. How could she have heard that voice?

"Lemme go, Auntie Trish!" Ramsay wiggled free of her locked arms, stumbled a few steps away and whirled to stare round-eyed at a point just behind Trish's shoulder.

"Ramsay," Trish forced a croak free of her suddenly dry mouth. "Ramsay, who is standing behind me?"

"Turn round and see for yourself, sweetling. Or have ye no' missed me?"

With a choking scream, Trish whirled round on the smooth stone bench and launched herself upward into a pair of muscular arms. Wrapping her legs around Maxwell's waist, she buried her face against the warmth of his neck and squeezed as hard as she could. *Please don't let this be a dream. Please don't let this be a cruel hallucination that's going to evaporate into the evening fog.* Eyes tightly shut, Trish inhaled a deep breath, reveling in the familiarity of Maxwell's spicy scent. If this was truly a trick of her mind, she prayed it would never end. "Please be real, please be real." Maybe if she whispered it aloud enough times, the Fates would make it so.

Maxwell's rumbling laughter shook through her as he spun her in his arms. "I am real, lass—as real as an ancient Highlander from the 1400s can be."

Trish held his face between her hands and touched the tip of her nose to his. "How? I thought you were...the headstone...the date."

Maxwell chuckled. "I believe if ye checked yon stone ye will find the date has disappeared." His eyes darkened and his face grew solemn as he pressed his forehead against hers. "All that remains on the stone is the inscription. Those words will never change."

Trish closed her eyes against the warm tears running down her cheeks. "I love you, Maxwell. I love you so much more than I ever thought possible. Please know how much I love you." Lordy, she couldn't say those words enough. She'd made the mistake of not saying the words before. She'd be damned if she'd make that mistake again.

Maxwell cut off her words with a hard claiming kiss as he held her even tighter. Pausing for just a moment with his lips still touching hers, Maxwell shuddered and whispered against her mouth. "And I love you more than life itself and I have come to claim ye as my bride."

Trish silenced him with another kiss. She longed to savor the taste of him. She thought she'd lost his sweetness forever.

"Mama. Are they ever gonna stop kissing?" Ramsay's bored voice echoed through the garden, followed by a chorus of tittering laughter.

Unbelievable joy surged through her and warmed the color to her cheeks. Trish peeped over Maxwell's shoulder at the MacKay family waiting at the edge of the garden. Her gaze settled on a familiar face. Another MacKay she had never thought she would see again. "Keagan?"

"Aye." Keagan nodded, his face beaming with a grin spreading from ear to ear.

A rush of guilt dampened her joy as Maxwell lowered Trish's feet to the ground. "Oh, Keagan. You'll never see your family again because of us. Now, you're forever trapped in the future."

Keagan's smile widened as he hooked his thumbs into the waist of his kilt and looked over at Latharn. After receiving Latharn's single nod, he moved a bit closer to Maxwell and Trish. "It sounds as though Uncle Latharn told ye about one of the MacKay gifts." Ducking his head, his expression softened as he stubbed the worn toe of his brown boot against the moss covered edge of one of the flagstones. "But Uncle Latharn didn't know until today that the MacKay magic is a bit different with me."

Confusion joined all the other emotions running amok in Trish's being. Holding tight to Maxwell's arms, she leaned against the security of his chest. She'd never let him go again. "What are you talking about, Keagan? Are you saying you get more than one free token when it comes to traveling through time?"

Keagan chuckled as Ramsay ran to his side and thumped him on the shoulder. "I'm still quite new to all the gifts my grandmothers granted me. But with mother's help, I've learned how to dance across the web of time and can do so as often as I like...as long as I have good reason."

"Your grandmothers?" Trish held a hand against her chest. If her heart beat any harder, it was surely going to break free of her body. Maxwell was here and if Trish understood Keagan, they even had a choice as to which time period they chose to live."

"Aye." Keagan nodded with a sheepish grin. "Mother told me we must always protect the secret of my ancestry but she gave me leave to share it with you. Goddess Brid and goddess Cerridwen are my grandmothers. They hold me close in their hearts and bless me with the Ways."

Maxwell stepped forward, pulling Keagan into a hug while keeping Trish locked against his side. "Thank ye, Keagan. I am forever in yer debt for reuniting me with my love."

Keagan's face grew suddenly serious as he retracted from Maxwell's embrace and stepped back to the center of the path. He first glanced toward the twenty-first century MacKays then turned his focus back to Maxwell and Trish.

Trish sensed an uneasiness about the boy. She read him as easily as Ramsay. "What do you need to tell us, Keagan? What's bothering you?"

Keagan shifted positions, first crossing his arms over his chest then returning his thumbs to their hooked position atop his kilt. "Your choice must be made. And it can only be made the once."

Maxwell pulled Trish tighter against his side. Trish dug her fingernails into Maxwell's arm. She'd be damned if she let anything separate them again. "What choice?"

Keagan nodded toward Trish's midriff then cleared his throat before he spoke. "Do the two of ye choose to raise your child in the past or shall ye tend your family here in the future? The choice is yours but take care with what ye choose, because I will only shift ye across the web the one time. I must not abuse the portal. The balance of the continuum canna be risked and I must guard its well-being."

Trish pressed her hands against her stomach. It wasn't possible. The doctors had said too much damage had been done. A large warm hand covered her own as a husky voice whispered into her hair. "Dinna doubt the boy, sweetling. He has the knowledge of an old soul. Keagan is never wrong."

Trish smiled; a warm aura of contentment filled her as she snuggled deeper into Maxwell's embrace. "Then *when* shall we raise this miraculous child of ours, my stubborn, burly Highlander?"

"I dinna care," Maxwell rumbled against her cheek. "As long as we raise the bairn together."

Trish closed her eyes, losing herself in Maxwell's delicious scent and warm comforting embrace. When? What time would she choose? The safe familiarity of the twenty-first century with all its conveniences and chaos or the rugged excitement of the past—the world where Maxwell truly belonged? Trish smiled as her heart swelled with the answer. Without opening her eyes, she tightened her arms around Maxwell's waist and whispered loud enough for Keagan to hear. "Take us home, Keagan. I belong with my Highlander in the past."

COMING SOON!

A Heartbeat Back to the Highlands
A MacKay Clan Legends
Ronan's Story
Book 5

MAEVEGREYSON.COM
Magical Romance Sifting Through Time

If you enjoyed this story, please consider leaving a review on the site where you purchased your copy, or a reader site such as Goodreads, or BookBub.

Visit my website at maevegreyson.com to sign up for my newsletter and stay up to date on new releases, sales, and all sorts of whatnot. (There are some freebies too!)

I would be nothing without my readers. You make it possible for me to do what I love. Thank you SO much!

Sending you big hugs and hoping you always have a great story to enjoy!

Maeve

About the Author

maevegreyson.com

USA Today Bestselling Author. Multiple RONE Award Winner. Multiple Holt Medallion Finalist.

Maeve Greyson's mantra is this: No one has the power to shatter your dreams unless you give it to them.

She and her husband of over forty years traveled around the world while in the U.S. Air Force. Now they're settled in rural Kentucky where Maeve writes about her courageous Highlanders and the fearless women who tame them. When she's not plotting the perfect snare, she can be found herding cats, grandchildren, and her husband—not necessarily in that order.

Also by Maeve Greyson

HIGHLAND PROTECTOR SERIES

Sadie's Highlander

Joanna's Highlander

Katie's Highlander

HIGHLAND HEARTS SERIES

My Highland Lover

My Highland Bride

My Tempting Highlander

My Seductive Highlander

THE MACKAY CLAN

Beyond A Highland Whisper

The Highlander's Fury

A Highlander In Her Past

OTHER BOOKS BY MAEVE GREYSON

Stone Guardian

Eternity's Mark

Guardian of Midnight Manor

When the Midnight Bell Tolls

THE SISTERHOOD OF INDEPENDENT LADIES

To Steal a Duke

To Steal a Marquess

To Steal an Earl

Printed in Great Britain
by Amazon

39659171R00066